Max Pulled Marisa Into His Arms And Hugged Her To Him.

If Marisa had learned nothing else about Max since she'd known him, she'd learned that he didn't like to be touched. Not by anybody. She was shocked to her toes by his action.

This was *Max,* the aloof and hard-to-know agent who did his job and went his own way. *Max*—the man who was all business and whose personal life remained a mystery, even to those closest to him. *Max,* the man she'd secretly coveted since the first day she'd met him . . .

He held her in his arms. The heat of him wrapped around her chilled and shivering body, warming her, beginning a blaze that went straight to the core of her.

The ensuing time was a blur. She didn't remember how they had ended up on the floor of the cave, their clothes forming a pallet of sorts. All she knew was how much she had dreamed about such a moment. She was living out all her most erotic and sensuous fantasies with the man of her dreams. . . .

Dear Reader,

Annette Broadrick fans (and you know who you all are!) rejoice. Annette's *Man of the Month, Where There Is Love,* is here! This is the story you've all been waiting for: superspy Max Moran *finally* meets his match! I'm not going to tell you a single thing about this fantastic book; you've just got to read it for yourselves.

May is also chock-full of books by authors I know you love. Let's start with BJ James's *Tears of the Rose,* written in BJ's uniquely unforgettable style. Next, Leslie Davis Guccione returns with *Rough and Ready,* a title that describes her hero perfectly!

Expect the unexpected in Joan Johnston's *A Little Time in Texas,* and thrill to Justine Davis's dramatic *Upon the Storm.* And last, but not least, is *Talk of the Town* by Beverly Barton, in which it's not just the weather that gets steamy in Riverton, Mississippi.

As for next month...well, you're all in for an exciting treat. Believe it or not, it's the ten-year anniversary of Silhouette Desire, which was launched back in June 1982. To celebrate, I've convinced six of your favorite Desire authors to participate in a very special program, JUNE GROOMS, in which six sinfully sexy heroes are saying goodbye to the single life—forever. Don't miss it!

All the best,

Lucia Macro
Senior Editor

ANNETTE BROADRICK

WHERE THERE IS LOVE

SILHOUETTE *Desire*®

Published by Silhouette Books New York

America's Publisher of Contemporary Romance

SILHOUETTE BOOKS
300 East 42nd St., New York, N.Y. 10017

WHERE THERE IS LOVE

ISBN: 0-373-05714-8

First Silhouette Books printing May 1992

Books by Annette Broadrick

Silhouette Desire

Hunter's Prey #185
Bachelor Father #219
Hawk's Flight #242
Deceptions #272
Choices #283
Heat of the Night #314
Made in Heaven #336
Return to Yesterday #360
Adam's Story #367
Momentary Marriage #414
With All My Heart #433
A Touch of Spring #464
Irresistible #499
A Loving Spirit #552
Candlelight For Two #577
Lone Wolf #666
Where There Is Love #714

Silhouette Romance

Circumstantial Evidence #329
Provocative Peril #359
Sound of Summer #412
Unheavenly Angel #442
Strange Enchantment #501
Mystery Lover #533
That's What Friends Are For #544
Come Be My Love #609
A Love Remembered #676
Married?! #742
The Gemini Man #796

Silhouette Books

Silhouette Christmas Stories 1988
"Christmas Magic"

ANNETTE BROADRICK

lives on the shores of Lake of the Ozarks in Missouri, where she spends her time doing what she loves most—reading and writing romance fiction. Since 1984, when her first book was published, Annette has been delighting her readers with her imaginative and innovative style. In addition to being nominated by *Romantic Times* magazine as one of the Best New Authors of 1984, she has also won the *Romantic Times* Reviewer's Choice Award for Best in its Series for her novels *Heat of the Night, Mystery Lover* and *Irresistible,* the *Romantic Times* WISH Award for her hero in *Strange Enchantment* and the *Romantic Times* Lifetime Achievement Award for Series Romance.

This book is dedicated to Ann Matthews Stroud,
a dear and close friend for forty-six years!
Here's to the next forty-six!

Prologue

———

Her blood pounded so loudly in her ears that she wasn't sure at first whether the noise she heard was her rapidly beating heart or footsteps striking a steady rhythm from somewhere behind her. She paused in her flight, holding her breath for a moment. Into the silence came the sound she had been dreading: heavy footsteps echoing on the cobbled street of the ancient city. She could no longer count on having eluded her pursuers.

She'd been out of the business for too long; her skills had grown rusty. She'd almost gotten herself killed earlier, and the danger was far from over. She was afraid to return to her hotel room because they might be waiting for her there.

Frantically she glanced around the darkened street, looking for a place to hide. She tried to reassure herself. Perhaps the person she heard approaching was only taking a shortcut home. *Please let it be so,* she whispered fervently. Please let him be a late-night reveler innocently wending his way home before dawn.

Even if the man approaching was not looking for her, she couldn't afford to be seen by anyone—not the way she was dressed. She glanced down at her frothy evening gown and frivolous dancing slippers. They made her much too conspicuous. She could be easily remembered and described. There was no safety for her at the moment other than to remain hidden.

She edged closer to a nearby building and pressed herself against the stuccoed wall where the darkest shadows offered hope for concealment. Her lungs ached from restraining the impulse to gasp for air. Instead, she forced herself to take small, shallow and soundless breaths while she waited to see who was approaching.

The footsteps never hesitated as he drew nearer to her. Still hidden, she began to relax. If he was following her, surely he would have approached the dark area with more caution.

Now he was just a few feet away from her, an indistinct form in the deep shadows. He passed her without breaking stride, continuing on his way as though familiar with his surroundings.

She waited until the streets were silent once more, then took a deep breath. So far, so good. There was no reason to panic, she reminded herself. She was a professional, after all, even if she hadn't worked in the field for six years.

She waited for her pulse to slow to a more normal rate before she ventured down the street once more.

All right. She was safe enough at the moment. What she needed to do now was to decide on a new plan of action. All of her previous plans would have to be discarded.

After considering her options she finally faced what she had to do, but she didn't like it. She would have to turn for help to the man she had spent the past six years avoiding.

Once again she studied the deserted street, looked down at her dress and gritted her teeth.

She really had no choice. The only thing left for her to do was to find a public telephone on a quiet street somewhere.

She could only pray that he wouldn't hang up on her!

One

———

Shrill ringing shattered the late-night silence. Max groped blindly for the telephone.

"H'lo." Sleep caused his normally gruff voice to sound more intimidating than usual.

"Max?"

The voice on the phone was too faint to identify, but he recognized the gender and the urgency. One of his agents must be in trouble.

He leaned over and flipped on the light beside his bed. It was close to midnight in Washington, D.C. Not late by some standards, but Max had had a rough day. He'd lost another operative, something that was happening with alarming frequency. He'd spent the day investigating the loss and had been in bed less than two hours, just long enough to have been deeply asleep.

"Who is this?"

A wave of static swept over the line as she answered. He had a sinking feeling that he was about to get some more bad news about one of his people.

He swung his legs over the side of the bed and sat up. As soon as the static wave receded, he spoke.

"I didn't catch your name. Will you please repeat it and tell me where you're calling from." He grabbed a pen and paper.

The next time she spoke, her voice was as clear as though she were standing in front of him.

"This is Marisa Stevens, Max. I'm in Barcelona. I know we didn't part on the best of terms, but I stumbled onto something tonight that's over my head. I could use your help."

When he realized who was calling, he felt as though he had been hit in the solar plexus. Memories immediately swirled through his mind. Emotions of all kinds were evoked by the mere sound of her voice. As though he'd seen her only yesterday, he pictured her face—wide-spaced green eyes, slightly tilted; a provocative smile that had always had the ability to curl his toes; and a mass of flaming red curls that gave mute evidence to a fiery and fiercely independent nature. A call for help was the last thing he ever expected to receive from Marisa Stevens.

"Tell me what you need."

"A change of clothes and a place to hide. I inadvertently overheard a conversation between two men who should not have been seen together. They're going to do whatever is necessary to make sure I don't live to repeat what I heard."

There was silence on the line for a moment before she continued. "I'm wearing an evening dress, and I'll look very conspicuous once people begin to stir in a couple of hours. I don't dare go back to my hotel room in case they're waiting for me there." There was a longer pause. "I need to get out of Spain, but I don't have a clue how to leave without being spotted."

He rubbed his forehead, forcing the last sleep from his brain. "Barcelona," he murmured, trying to think of a safe place for her to go. A face flashed in his mind. Santiago had originally come from a small fishing village on the coast not far from Barcelona. Max had been there on more than one occasion to meet with Santiago.

"Marisa? There's a woman I know in that area who will help you." He gave her instructions and directions to the fishing village. "I haven't heard from Teresa in a couple of years, not since her son, Santiago, died, but I'm sure she'll help you. Since she doesn't have a phone, I can't call her and alert her to your situation. When you get there explain that I sent you and told you to wait until someone contacts you."

"Thank you, Max. I really appreciate this."

"What are you doing in Spain?"

"It's a long story."

"You haven't worked in our business for years and Spain is a long way from Seattle. What's happened to put you in danger?"

There was a small pause. "I wasn't aware you knew where I was or what I was doing."

"I've always known, Marisa."

There was another pause. Then Max spoke again. "You haven't answered my question. I need to know what's going on if I'm going to help."

"I was trying to contact a man from Seattle. I'd followed him to Barcelona. Before I could approach him directly I inadvertently overheard a conversation between him and a man I used to know years ago. Their conversation was rather incriminating. When I attempted to get away from them they heard me, and I'm afraid they recognized me."

"Can you name names?"

"The man I'm following is Troy Chasen. It's a personal matter. The other one is a former agent. We worked together on a couple of assignments."

"His name?"

"Harry O'Donnell."

"Harry is still with the Agency, Marisa."

"Oh, Lord, then it's worse than I thought!"

"What do you mean?"

"They were planning a shipment of goods. From their reaction when they discovered I was there, I assume the stuff is contraband."

"Thanks for the information, Marisa. It could be invaluable on a matter I've been dealing with for some time. I'll follow up to see what more I can find out."

"I still have to find Troy."

"Even if he sees you as a threat now?"

She sighed. "I can't just give up. This is too important."

"Maybe I can help you."

"No! I really think I can handle this one on my own."

"Then why did you call me?"

"What I mean is, if you can get me out of Spain, I can contact Troy. They were talking about another meeting in Nice. Once I've spoken to him and gotten the necessary information from him, I'll promise to stay out of his life."

"If he's smuggling, I have a hunch he won't shake your hand and wave you a cordial goodbye, Marisa. You know better than that."

He caught the hint of a sob in her voice. "I have to try, Max. I can't give up on this one. Thanks for your help." She hung up before he could say anything more.

Max stared frustratedly at the phone he continued to hold in his hand. She could be the most aggravating, irritating, bullheaded agent he'd ever worked with, and that was saying something! He should have been glad she quit the Agency, glad she moved across the continent from him.

He slammed down the phone and reached for a cigar. In the course of one rather short conversation he had just learned the name of at least one of the possible traitors in the group as well as the name of a man who might be part of the smuggling ring his unit had been tracking for years. Marisa could very well have stumbled onto the key that would open several doors to apprehending the perpetrators.

Troy Chasen. Marisa had said her business with him was personal. What in the hell was she mixed up in?

And why did he care?

He turned away from that last thought. Whatever had been between them had ended abruptly six years ago. He wasn't very proud of the way he'd handled the situation. It was the only time in his career when he had lost his objectivity and his professionalism, both necessary for an agent's survival.

The irony of his subsequent promotion had not escaped him. By then the damage had been done—he'd already become emotionally involved with her. The damage could not be undone.

After six years she was back in his life, if only temporarily. He hoped he'd gained some perspective during those years.

He glanced at his watch. It was almost one o'clock in the morning, but he needed some answers. If Harry had turned, then the work they'd been doing had been compromised. A slow rage began to build within him. There was nothing more lethal than an agent gone bad.

And it looked as though Marisa was right in the middle of a deadly situation.

Several hours later Max sat across the desk from his superior. This was the man who had peremptorily recalled Max from the field six years before and put him in charge of their special unit. Max thought of him by the nickname of "Obi-wan," a character in a famous science-fiction movie series who had a habit of appearing in spirit form to characters in the movie during a time of great danger, offering advice and building their morale.

At the moment Max could definitely use some advice. The information he'd gathered during the past several hours had been daunting.

After twenty years in the business, he wondered if he was losing his grip. How could he have missed what now seemed so obvious, once some of the missing pieces had been supplied?

He had begun by reviewing Harry's reports to the Agency over the past three years. Now that he knew what he was looking for, a pattern began to emerge. Harry had given him bogus information that kept his operatives away during times when shipments were made. Every time an agent came too close, he was eliminated.

Max had tapped into classified government files to find out everything he could about Troy Chasen. He had learned a great deal about this man's financial situation. Chasen was a very successful business-man whose import-export headquarters were located in Seattle, Washington, but all his business operations looked legal.

He still hadn't found the connection between Chasen and Marisa, and he didn't like the direction his thoughts were taking. Would she have given him the potentially incriminating evidence about Chasen if she was having an affair with the man? She could have changed a great deal these past few years. He didn't know, but he was damned well going to find out.

"You requested this meeting, Max," Obi-wan stated, making it clear that he didn't want his time wasted.

"Yes, sir. I received information late last night that sheds some light on what's been happening to some of my agents."

"Is your source reliable?"

"I'd say so. It was Marisa Stevens. She used to be with the Agency."

"Marisa. Hmm. Your last assignment in the field was with Marisa, wasn't it?"

Since the man had a photographic memory, Max considered the question to be rhetorical, but answered anyway. "Yes, sir."

"She left soon after your promotion."

"Yes."

"Why?"

"Because I wouldn't give her any more field assignments."

"Why?"

"Because I felt she could better serve the Agency as an analyst in her field of expertise."

"Which is?"

"Southeast Asian culture."

"She disagreed?"

"Yes. She insisted that she preferred to work in the field. I refused to send her. She resigned." Max forced himself to remain perfectly still.

"What has she been doing since that time?"

"According to our file, she moved to Seattle, went back to school for her doctorate and has been teaching at the university there."

"How would Marisa stumble across information that would implicate one of our agents?"

"She's in Spain and accidentally ran into Harry O'Donnell there, where he had no business being.

She overheard a conversation that was incriminating."

"Why do you suppose Marisa called you, her former recalcitrant boss, to report a traitor in the ranks? Is she feeling more charitable toward you these days?"

"Not so you'd notice," Max replied wryly. "I'm not fully apprised of her situation. But I intend to be before long."

"O'Donnell, is it? Well, well." Obi-wan's brows arched. "No wonder you've had trouble pinning our phantom down." He placed his fingers in a precise steeple and studied them. "I'm sorry to hear your news, Max. He's one of the best."

"Yes."

"So what do you intend to do about it?"

"Go after him."

"How?"

"At the present time, Marisa is safely hidden away in a small fishing village on the Spanish coast. I want to get her out of there and back to the States. Then I intend to go to Nice and confront Harry."

"Alone?"

"If necessary."

"As laudable as your plan is—my God! I can see you now, galloping in to save the day—I need you here, Max. Send someone else."

"I thought of that, sir. At the moment, I don't know who I can trust. Harry might not be working alone."

"Hmm." The man sat there for a few moments, studying Max. "I suppose I can spare you for a few days."

"Then you agree that I should go?"

"Let's just say that I don't disagree with your assessment of the situation. You're good at what you do. If anyone can outsmart Harry, you can. This is a very touchy situation. A breach of national security is always a nasty business. Whoever got to Harry has a great deal of clout. We can't underestimate these people."

"I never have."

"I know. That's why I have you in your present position. Be sure you make it safely back to continue."

"Yes, sir." Max came to his feet, relieved that he'd accomplished his goal.

"Oh, and Max. Give my regards to Marisa."

Two

———

Max waited until almost midnight before he had two of the fishing trawler's crew lower one of its small boats and row him to shore. He was thankful there was no moon. He was also thankful that he was still familiar enough with the shoreline along this part of Spain to recall the seldom-used cove where they were heading.

Long after the two crew members had left him on the deserted shore, Max waited, watching to see if he had been observed disembarking from the small craft. Once he was certain that no one had seen him, he searched for and found the path that led to the roadway above.

He glanced at the glowing dial of his watch, now set for local time. He should reach Teresa's small cottage a couple of hours after sunrise.

The sun had been above the horizon almost three hours by the time Max reached the outskirts of the small fishing village where Teresa lived.

Teresa's cottage hadn't changed much, but her garden was growing wild, uncared for. That wasn't like Teresa. He let himself into the back gate and moved quietly up to the door that he knew opened directly into the kitchen. Teresa should be there by now preparing breakfast. He hoped everything was all right.

He tapped lightly on the wooden door. When there was no answer after a moment or two, he tapped a little harder. A whisper in Spanish asked who was there. In equally soft Spanish, he replied,

"It's Max, Teresa. May I come in?"

The long silence after his announcement worried him. He reached for the revolver at the small of his back.

The door swung open and a figure stepped into the morning sunlight. Max relaxed.

"What in the world are *you* doing here?"

"Hello, Marisa."

She stood before him in an unadorned white cotton blouse and black skirt. Her red hair seemed to catch fire in the sunlight.

He'd been prepared to see her and still it was a shock to him, so he could imagine how she must feel. He stood there staring at her, looking for any differences in her appearance.

She was still beautiful. All of the familiar responses swept over him and he mentally cursed.

Marisa couldn't seem to adjust to the sudden shock of Max's appearance. He'd told her that someone would contact her. Never in her wildest imaginings had she thought it would be Max himself.

He wore a black T-shirt that snugly fitted across his broad shoulders and muscular arms. Black jeans molded his trim waist, taut buttocks and muscular thighs. He still wore his brown hair short, almost military in style, and his sherry-colored eyes had not lost their mesmerizing quality. Those eyes had haunted her through the years.

She had hoped that time had changed him, that sitting behind a desk had softened his body, made him less dangerous looking. The only change she could see was a hint of silver around his temples. He continued to radiate a raw sexuality that seemed to reach into a part of her that she had kept determinedly locked away. In the six years since she'd seen him, no man had gotten close to her. One look at Max and she could feel a tight coil deep inside her beginning to unwind, leaving her prey to her deepest emotions.

Max stepped inside with a lithe movement and closed the door behind him. His quick glance encompassed the kitchen before he asked, "Where's Teresa?"

"She isn't here."

He returned his gaze to the woman who stood so stiffly before him. With a slightly lifted brow, he asked, "Then how did you get in?"

Marisa realized that she felt defensive and forced herself to say calmly, "She was here when I arrived yesterday morning. She'd come to check on the place before returning to her sister's home in the hills. Her sister has been quite ill and Teresa's been looking after her family. When I explained my situation, she invited me to stay as long as necessary. I assured her that I could look after myself. She plans to return at the end of the week."

"We'll be leaving tomorrow night."

That meant that she would be there alone with Max, a situation Marisa wanted to avoid at all costs. "Why can't we leave tonight?"

Max could see that very little had changed between them. She was going to challenge everything he said. Well, he would have to make the best of the situation that he'd helped to create. He turned away and walked over to the stove where he found a pot of coffee. He poured himself a cup before he answered, hoping the delay would give him a stronger grip on his impatience with her fractious attitude.

"I wasn't sure of the situation here or how long it would take to get to and from the point of rendezvous. To be on the safe side, I gave us an extra day." He took a sip of his coffee, then went over to the small table and sat down. "In the meantime, you can brief me on exactly what happened to you and why."

"Why isn't important. I was—"

His control wavered. "The hell it isn't. I don't give a damn about your personal life, sweetheart, but you *will* tell me exactly what is going on. I'll decide what's important." She stood in the middle of the floor, watching him warily. With poorly concealed irritation, he pointed to the chair across from him. "Sit down."

Marisa could feel her temper flaring at his peremptory order. After a slow count to ten, she said, "I no longer work for you, Max." Despite her words, Marisa walked over and sat where he had indicated.

"Oh, I'm very aware of that, Marisa. You moved clear across the continent to get away from me." He caught the tinge of bitterness in his voice and was irritated with himself.

"Not you, Max."

"That isn't the way I saw it."

"I just knew that the situation wasn't going to work. It was one thing for us to work together on equal terms. It was another matter when you were given authority over me."

Max leaned back in his chair and studied the woman across from him. "Was it me personally, or do you resent taking orders from any man?" he drawled.

She gave him a level look. "That's a rather low blow, isn't it, Max?"

He shrugged, feeling slightly ashamed of himself. "Maybe."

"I never resented being given orders. I followed them implicitly. I was a good agent, but that didn't seem to matter to you. You refused to let me go back out in the field."

He glanced down at the cup he held in his hands. Without meeting her eyes, he muttered, "I had my reasons."

"What were they?"

"They no longer matter, if they ever did." He glanced up and said, "Chasen's married, you know," watching to see if he would get a reaction.

Her amused grin caught him off guard.

"As a matter of fact, Max, I was there when he got married."

She'd turned the tables on him. He was caught totally unprepared. He stared at her, unable to comment.

After a moment, she relented, saying, "He's married to my sister Eileen."

"Your sister!"

"That's right."

Why hadn't he known that? She'd gone to Seattle after she resigned and stayed with her sister. Her sister had been single at the time. He mulled the information over in his mind for several minutes before he asked,

"Do you think Chasen is using his import-export business as a front?"

She was quiet, obviously thinking as she gazed out the window beside the table. "I never thought so before," she eventually admitted in a slow voice. Turning to look at Max, she said, "Now, I don't know what to think."

He leaned forward, staring at her intently. "Tell me exactly what happened to you the other night."

Feeling suddenly restless, she got up from her chair and began to pace.

"Eileen and Troy have not been getting along for several months. He's been gone a great deal lately. Whenever he came home they fought about his schedule. After one of their fights he stormed out of the house, saying he wasn't coming back. She was upset and crying, of course. She went on to bed and waited for him. He never showed up again.

"The next morning she went in to check on Timmy and discovered he was gone."

"Timmy?"

She turned away from him and walked over to the window. Gazing at the flowers, she muttered, "Her son."

"Chasen's records don't show that he has a son."

"No. Because Timmy isn't his."

"I see. But you think that Chasen took him, anyway?"

She turned away from the window and looked at him. "I don't know. He and Timmy have a good relationship, but it makes no sense to me. That's why I came after Troy. I think he's playing games with Eileen. I don't know. Nobody seemed to have heard anything from either of them. I couldn't sit around and wait for answers, so I decided to go after him."

"Does Chasen know your background?"

"No. He knows I worked in Washington after I finished college, but he's never shown any interest in what I did there."

"Obviously he didn't expect you to follow him."

"No. It took some effort to find out that he'd come to Spain. When I did, I flew here immediately, hoping either to locate Troy or find someone who knew him. I have some friends whose relatives live here. They've often suggested that I look them up, so I did. When they invited me to attend a rather grand reception, I agreed to go because I thought I might meet someone there who knew Troy."

"So what happened?"

"I was at the party and was returning from the ladies' room when I rounded a corner and recognized Troy's voice. He was talking with someone and heading toward me. I decided to wait until he was alone to confront him, so I darted through the first door I saw, thinking I'd wait until after they passed. Instead of continuing down the hallway, they came into the room where I was. I barely managed to hide behind the draperies before they turned on a lamp and continued their conversation.

"It was while I was waiting for them to leave that I realized I recognized the second man, as well. It was Harry. They were discussing a shipment and how difficult it was becoming not to get caught. Troy said something like, 'What about Jameson?' and Harry replied, 'Don't worry about him. I'll take care of him just like I did the others.'"

"A chill went through me at his tone of voice. At first when I recognized Harry I assumed that Troy was helping the government apprehend the smugglers. After Harry's remarks, I knew better. I also knew that I had to get out of there before either of them spotted me. I eased the window open and crawled outside. My shoe must have scraped against the stucco, because they stopped talking. Harry jerked the drapes aside just as I let go of the windowsill and dropped to the hedge below. I got only a quick look at his face, but I saw anger, recognition and determination. Believe me, I didn't hang around after that. I ran until I was far enough away to feel safe. Then I called you."

"As soon as I get you out of here, I'm going to Nice. As far as Harry will know, I'm on vacation.

While I'm there I'll see what I can find out about Troy and your nephew."

"I want to go with you."

"No."

"Max!"

"You're no longer a part of the Agency, Marisa."

"Fine. Then you can't tell me what to do."

"I sure as hell can. You're a private citizen who had no business getting involved in this matter."

"That's nonsense, and you know it. I'm already involved. Why, you wouldn't even know about Harry if I hadn't contacted you."

"And you were in over your head or you wouldn't have called me."

"So? All that means is that together we can deal with this situation. We've worked together before, Max. We can do it again."

"Absolutely not!"

"Oh! You are the most infuriating, obstinate, arrogant man I've ever had the misfortune to be around."

"I seem to recall hearing similar sentiments the last time I saw you."

"I hoped you had changed over the years, mellowed a little. Hah!"

"If anything, you're more beautiful than I remembered," he said in a husky voice.

She'd been pacing, obviously trying to get a grip on her temper. When he spoke she came to an abrupt halt and stared at him suspiciously. "Why did you say that?"

He looked at her in surprise. "I don't know. I guess I was thinking out loud."

She came toward him and leaned her palms on the table. "Max, you've got to let me do this. What if Troy has Timmy with him? You don't want any harm to come to an innocent child, do you?"

"Of course not! I'm not a monster, Marisa. How old is the boy?"

She straightened. "Why do you ask?"

Impatiently, he said, "Because his age has a great deal to do with how I handle the matter."

"He's five," she stated in a flat voice.

"Are you close to him?"

"Yes."

"Then you wouldn't have any trouble getting him to go with you if we did find him."

"None whatsoever."

"I'll think about it."

She started to say something, then closed her mouth and spun away from the table.

Max knew that he needed to get away from Marisa for a while. Being around her once again was taking its toll on his ability to control his feelings and his reactions to her. "I think I'm going outside for a while to work on Teresa's garden. She could use some help around here."

"That sounds like a spectacular idea. I'm tired of pacing in here, waiting. That's all I've done for the past day and night."

So much for getting away from her. At least outside he could distance himself from her. He started toward the door. "You were never very patient."

"I can be, when there's a need for it. Waiting to be spirited out of the country has been nerve-racking, I'll admit. I guess I've lost my edge."

She followed him outside and watched as he gathered the shears and flower clippers. He handed her the clippers, then walked away, moving over to the front gate.

"This really feels strange," she said after they had worked for more than an hour without saying anything.

Max paused in his trimming and removed his shirt, then wiped the perspiration from his face with the large handkerchief he pulled from his back pocket. Only then did he look around at Marisa and ask, "What are you talking about?"

"We've known each other a long time. We worked together; we've been in some really dangerous places together; and yet we've never done anything quite so domestic as working together in a garden."

"That's not surprising. In my line of work, I don't get much of a chance to be domestic."

"Have you ever thought about giving it up?" she asked, pulling weeds about three feet from where he worked on the hedge.

"No," he said immediately, not having to think about his answer. "It's what I do. Why? Do you miss it?"

She took her time in replying. "Not really, and that does surprise me. What I came to realize was that I'd become addicted to the adrenaline rush that comes when you know your life is on the line. By the time I decided to go back to school I knew that I no longer needed that kind of excitement in my life."

"So why didn't you come back and work in the Agency again?"

"You mean, in the job you offered?"

"Yes."

"I didn't figure you'd want me. I felt that was the reason you offered it to me in the first place, so that I would quit."

He stopped what he was doing and turned to face her. "You really believed that?"

"What other reason could you have had? I was good at what I did. I knew that. So did you. But for some reason you no longer wanted me around."

"No! That wasn't true at all! Dammit, you know the training. You can't afford to get close to anyone in this business. You can't afford to make friends. It can get you killed. After our last assignment, I'd lost my objectivity where you were concerned. I explained all of that to you during that night we spent together. I thought you understood. I knew that I would never be able to be assigned a job with you again. Then I was called back to Washington and promoted." He turned away from her, forcing himself to concentrate on trimming the bushes around the front gate instead of the woman kneeling so gracefully in the flowerbed. "I could no longer send you out in the field," he admitted in a low voice. "I could no longer risk your life or take a chance on losing you." With bitter irony he added, "As it turned out, I lost you, anyway, but at least you were safe."

When she didn't say anything after several minutes, Max risked a glance over his shoulder. She was still kneeling, with her head bent. While he watched, she made a swipe across her cheek with her grimy hand. "Why didn't you tell me this six years ago, Max?" she muttered in an angry tone.

"I didn't think I had to, not after the night we'd spent together."

She glanced up at him and he saw the pain on her dirt-smeared face. "How was I supposed to know how you felt about that night? You never made reference to it again."

He rested his hands on his hips. "Just when would I have had an opportunity? If you will recall, we were immediately flown back to the States where I was informed that I would take over another position. I had a crash course in learning a new job. You certainly didn't make things any easier at the time, insisting that I send you out again."

"Well, I got bored sitting around with nothing to do but to wait for an assignment."

"I told you that we would talk about it, remember?"

"Your idea of 'talking about it' was to tell me that you wanted to put me behind a desk."

"You never gave me a chance to explain further. You blew up and ended up walking out of the office. I got your resignation in the mail two days later."

Their voices continued to rise until they were practically shouting at each other.

Max didn't want to remember the pain and intense loss he'd felt when he received her notice of resignation, to become effective immediately.

The sudden silence between them seemed to ring with suppressed emotions. Max could hear the buzzing of an insect in one of the flowers, the sound of distant voices down the roadway.

When she spoke, he barely heard her words. "I wish I'd known."

Her voice sounded so wistful that he could only look at her in surprise. "You mean it would have made a difference to you?"

"Oh, yes," she whispered, her eyes filled with painful memories of decisions made and losses suffered. "All the difference in the world."

Three

Marisa lay on a narrow bed in one of Teresa's upstairs bedrooms, unable to sleep. She had pounded and reshaped her pillow until it threatened to burst its seams. She had kicked off her covers, pulled them back up to her chin and now lay with them wrapped around one leg, leaving the other exposed beneath a short cotton nightgown.

All she could think about was her desperate need for sleep. Well, that's what she *wanted* to think about—going to sleep. What she *didn't* want to think about was Max lying across the hall in the other bedroom, in the other narrow bed, sound asleep.

She had spent the better part of the day making certain that she didn't look directly at him, particularly while he worked outside without his shirt.

Without his shirt, what had only been hinted at before had been blatantly revealed. She hadn't needed the reminder, hadn't needed to know how she still reacted to the man, regardless of the years that had elapsed since she had last seen him.

Marisa sighed. Max had always reminded her of a caged panther. Although he looked tame enough, and he acted tame enough, there was always something about him that made her feel he might spring at any moment—a coiled restlessness just beneath the surface.

Now as she lay twisted in her bedclothes, she recalled her strong reaction when he had arrived so unexpectedly at Teresa's door that morning. Nothing had changed for her. She had a hunch that nothing ever would.

She remembered the very first time she'd seen him. She had worked for the Agency for only a few weeks when there had been a briefing to announce that a small, very special unit was being formed to gather information on several activities that were strongly affecting the United States: the taking of hostages, illegal trading in guns and drugs, and the smuggling of artifacts into the United States.

Max had walked into the room that morning in conversation with another agent. She had noticed him right away, which surprised her when she thought about him later that night. The room had been filled with many men. He looked too rugged to be considered handsome, too tough to be gentle, too hard to admit to human emotions. And yet…and yet there was something about him that continually drew her eye to him. He appeared tall, even though he was little more than average height. He had the build of a runner or a swimmer and moved with a natural athlete's grace.

She never forgot him, even though it was months later when Marisa was formally introduced to Max.

The head of the division had introduced them, adding, "Marisa will keep you on your toes, Max. She graduated head of her class at our special training school. There are a great many diverse talents packed away in that petite body."

Max had nodded but ignored the hand she had offered him. "How long have you been with the Agency?"

"Almost six months now," she said, smiling.

He didn't return her smile. "And you're going to be part of this unit?" He glanced at the other man in surprise. When the division head didn't say anything, Max returned his attention to Marisa. "Don't you think you'd like a little more experience under your belt before you join a special unit?"

She shrugged, a little nettled by his attitude. "Obviously someone must have believed that I was

qualified, or I wouldn't have been offered the job."
She was doing her best to hold on to her temper.

Max either didn't notice her anger or ignored it.
His next question was more in the nature of an interrogation than social conversation. "Are you aware that we may be working together from time to time?"

Why did he have to make it sound as though she'd only recently been hatched from an egg? Determined to keep her cool and retain the semblance of a polite facade, Marisa limited her response.

"Yes."

"I won't be in a position to train a rookie," he warned brusquely.

That did it! Marisa gave him her loveliest smile and said, "Neither will I."

The division head laughed. "That will be the least of your worries, Marisa. Max has been with the Agency for years."

She glanced back at Max, deliberately widening her eyes in awe. "Really? And how's your reaction time? I don't want to be slowed down, you know."

What amazed her was that Max laughed, really laughed. His sherry-colored eyes, which had been studying her with a glacial glint just moments before, now filled with warm and wicked light. They gleamed with amusement.

"All right," he admitted with a grin, "so maybe I *was* coming on a little strong."

"A little? I was expecting you to send me back to the nursery and forbid me to associate with the adults."

They parted with a truce of sorts. During the next few years she worked with several agents, Max included. She learned a great deal during those years, about herself as well as about her chosen profession.

She *had* been green and much too naive when she'd first started, but she had managed to survive while she was learning.

By the time she and Max were assigned to follow up reports of drug running in Southeast Asia, she knew her strengths and her limitations. More than eighteen months had passed since their last assignment together. Max had taken the lead—not because he was male but because he was the senior agent. Max had always made it clear that he wouldn't make any allowances for her, and she respected him for that.

As usual for Max, he had kept his distance from her, dealing with her on a professional basis only. She didn't mind. He was one of the best agents they had. She had considered it a privilege to work with him.

Marisa had wondered if his excellence as an agent was one of the reasons they were placed together on this particular assignment. Had his concern for her as a woman been reflected in a similar way by their superior? Did the boss think Max could compensate for any lack she might show on an assignment?

She never knew because she never had the courage to confront her superior with her suspicions. She wanted the job too badly to risk such a confrontation.

For a moment her mind leaped to the last heated discussion between her and Max after he'd been promoted. She'd really blown it that day. She'd lost control over her temper and said to him all the things she'd harbored since she had taken the job. It was no wonder that he thought she was holding him responsible for everything that had happened to her since she'd joined the Agency. She'd certainly made it sound that way!

She still cringed with embarrassment at the way she'd left his office, storming out of there like some beleaguered Brunhilde. By the time she calmed down she had faced what she had done. Because of what happened between them during that last assignment, Max was certain to feel that she was using their intimacy as leverage to throw her weight around. Just thinking about it made her squirm with embarrassment.

She'd done the only thing possible. She'd mailed her resignation and run, going into hiding like some burrowing animal into the safety of its earth home.

Well, now Max was back in her life, at least temporarily. Would she have called him for help if she had known that he would come after her himself? There was no way to know, of course. She now had to play out this particular hand and see what happened.

Once again Marisa kicked off the sheet across her lower body and flopped over onto her stomach. She prayed for sleep, chanted brief phrases to convince herself that she was truly sleepy and attempted to make her mind blank. Her traitorous mind responded by recalling in exquisite detail the one night she most wanted to forget—the night everything went wrong on their assignment....

Marisa stayed on the cliffs overlooking the cove in accordance with Max's instructions. For a week they had been playing tourist along the coast of east Malaysia, scouting the area where, according to their sources, a large drug shipment was to be brought from the interior for distribution to various parts of the world.

Their job was to find out exactly where and when the drugs were to arrive and how and by whom they were to be shipped out. They were to share this information with local authorities and help to map out a strategy to capture the leaders of the operation.

Max had positioned himself close to the water, in one of the many outcroppings along the rugged beach. It was a precarious spot at best because of the tide.

Marisa waited and watched through binoculars. When the firing began she realized that someone knew exactly where Max was and that he was the victim of an ambush.

She never remembered later going down the steep cliffs. All she ever recalled was firing on the three men, catching *them* off guard and giving Max a chance to slip out of his hiding place and run toward the bluffs. She joined him and they raced along the sand in the shadow of the cliffs.

Unfortunately they were being followed, which was an easy enough task since they were leaving footprints in the dampened sand.

As it turned out, the tide that they had been so concerned about ended up saving their lives. As it came ever higher they were forced to search along the bluffs for an escape route. What they found was a well-concealed cave whose entrance was totally covered by water during high tide.

Max pointed out that just inside the entrance the cave began to climb higher. They had run out of time. The water prevented them from going any farther on the beach. They had to take their chances in the cave.

"I feel fresh air coming from somewhere up ahead," Max said. "So there's got to be a way out of here. C'mon." With a small flashlight, he led the way. She scrambled to keep up.

The passage continued to narrow until Marisa was convinced they could go no farther, but Max kept moving. Eventually they were rewarded when the pathway widened and they found themselves in a glowing underground room. The glow came from the phosphorescent rock that made up the walls of the cathedrallike area.

"Look!" Max pointed upward.

Marisa's gaze followed his gesture. The ceiling of the area was, in her estimate, at least thirty feet above them. In the middle of it was a ragged opening, at least three feet wide. From where they stood, they were able to see the night sky and the twinkling stars.

"Where are we? Do you know?" she whispered.

Max shook his head. "Not really."

"Will someone be able to look down and see us?"

"If they know about the opening and where it leads, I suppose they can." He looked around the area. "But they'd have a tough time getting to us from there." He touched some rubble nearby with his toe. "I would guess that more than one unsuspecting animal has fallen to its death."

She shivered.

"With any luck, those guys will think we drowned."

"Either that, or they'll be waiting for us at the entrance of the cave when we emerge at low tide."

He had been walking the perimeter of the airy rock room. He came to an abrupt halt at her words.

"Well, aren't you a shining tower of optimism tonight."

She stiffened. "I'm just being realistic, Max. You were almost killed out there."

He strolled back to where she stood. "That's quite true. I didn't have a chance until you showed up, guns ablazing."

"One gun, Max. That's all."

"One was enough. Thanks for saving my butt."

"That's what I was there for."

He grinned. "Well, you certainly performed your duties well." Now that he was standing so much closer she realized that his calm voice had deceived her about his mood. He was still keyed up, adrenaline still coursing through his body.

In a totally unexpected and uncharacteristic gesture, Max pulled her into his arms and hugged her to him.

If Marisa had learned nothing else about Max since she'd known him, she had learned that he didn't like to be touched. Not by anybody. She was shocked to her toes.

This was Max, the aloof and hard-to-know agent who did his job and went his own way.

Max, who was all business and whose personal life remained a mystery, even to those closest to him.

Max, the man she had secretly desired since the first day she'd met him.

Max held her in his arms. The heat of him wrapped around her chilled and shivering body, warming her, began a blaze that went straight to the core of her.

The ensuing moments were a blur. She recalled scattered moments: his lips scalding hers with passion; her arms tightening around him in a convulsive grasp; fumbling with his jacket and shirt in an effort to find his bare skin so that she could rub her hands over his back and chest in a frenzy of exploration.

He felt wonderful to the sensitive tips of her fingers and her palms ... firm and muscled ... smooth skin covering a well-honed body.

She didn't remember how they had ended up on the floor of the cave, their clothes forming a crude pallet of sorts. All she knew was how much she had dreamed about such a moment. She was living out all of her most erotic and sensuous fantasies with the man of her dreams.

He wasted no time claiming her. She clutched him in a frantic embrace, urging him on, until the fire that he had begun had grown from a tiny flame deep within her to a conflagration that consumed her entirely.

Long after the fire began to ebb with only an occasional spark as a reminder of what they had shared, he continued to hold her in his arms, his chin resting on the top of her head, which lay on his chest.

Never in her life had Marisa felt so at peace. She was drifting off to sleep when Max spoke.

"This has to be one of the most stupidly unprofessional things I have ever done," he said in a disgusted voice.

Marisa was glad he couldn't see her amusement at his tone of voice, which was a far cry from the gentle way he held her.

When she didn't answer, he went on. "Don't get me wrong, honey. I've wanted to jump your bones since the first time I saw you, but I knew better than to entertain the idea then, and I thought I'd tamped down all those erotic thoughts since."

Although his words sounded harsh, his voice was mellow. Hearing him admit to feelings much like those she had experienced over the years was at once reassuring and revealing. Perhaps not all the tension between them had been due to his reluctance to have her as his partner.

Marisa raised her head from its very comfortable pillow and brushed her lips across his.

"What was that for?"

"For letting me know how you feel," she whispered.

"I'm irritated as hell, and you're pleased about it?" he demanded to know.

"Max, you are a human being. Why are you working so diligently to be perfect?"

"Hah. I'm far from perfect. Anyone who knows me is aware of that."

"But who is that, Max?"

"What do you mean?"

"Who knows you? You keep yourself so aloof from everyone." Her hand continued to rest on his chest so that she felt his heart rate increase. She waited—almost holding her breath—for him to say something—to say anything—that would allow her to get to know him better.

"There's a suburb in Southern California with several foster families who know more than they want to know about me."

"Tell me, Max. Tell me about that time in your life."

He was quiet for so long that she was certain he had no intention of saying another word. He had begun moving his hand up and down her spine in a slow, lazy fashion. When he started speaking his voice was very soft, softer than she had ever heard it, so soft that she could almost see the young boy he described. She could hear the child as he described his pain.

"I had just finished the first grade that summer. I'd been let out to summer pasture and I was making the most of it. We had a typical tract home on a street lined with large shade trees. The area was a paradise for young boys who loved to climb trees and play in tree houses. Our next-door neighbors had two boys, one a year older, the other almost a year younger than I was. They had a tree house that my dad had helped their dad build for us. It was something else. We loved it. We spent all the time we could up there, spying on the world from our leaf-hidden eyrie.

"I was up there one morning when my mom called me to come home and clean up. They were going to town to do some shopping. I climbed down and went running to convince her to let me stay home and play with the neighbors.

"I remember her looking at my dad and communicating in that nonverbal way they had. As hard as I tried I couldn't tell how they did it. I never could read anything in their expressions, but she could ask and he could answer without a word being said. She said she'd check with our neighbor to make sure she didn't mind keeping an eye on me while they were gone. I knew she'd do it. She and Mom always traded off like that.

"Mom was getting Amanda dressed. My sister was fourteen months old, and reminded me of an animated doll. She had great big blue eyes...so blue they looked like they were painted on...and golden-white curls that bobbed on her head because she was never still for a minute, unless she was sound asleep. God! I loved to play with her. She thought I was so funny. As soon as I walked into the room she'd laugh out loud at me. Of course that encouraged me to clown around a lot, just to hear her laughter echoing in the house.

"I remember that she grabbed for my hand while Mom was trying to hold her still and Mom said, 'Don't play with her now, son. I'm trying to get her changed and dressed.'

"My dad tousled my hair and asked me if I wanted to go fishing with him the next morning. I loved going anywhere with my dad. I said 'Sure.' He reminded me that we had to get up really early. He always reminded me of that, as though I'd change my mind. It was kind of a game with us.

"So I waved goodbye, standing there in the driveway, watching them back out into the street. Everyone waved back, including Amanda, bouncing in her car seat between them."

He stopped speaking. Marisa had felt his muscles tensing during the telling of the story. Because she was once again lying with her head on his chest, she was aware when he swallowed, then swallowed a second time before saying in a monotone, "I never saw them again. They left that morning planning their day, expecting their lives to continue on indefinitely, but it didn't work out that way." He choked on the last word and just lay there in silence.

"What happened, Max?" The words were little more than a wisp of sound in the echoing cavern, but she knew that he heard them.

"It was one of those freak things you hear about. They had driven onto the main artery that fed traffic onto the freeway. They had just entered the freeway when a car changed three lanes at a high speed in an effort to elude a police car. They just happened to be in the wrong place at the wrong time, that's all. They were hit from behind and went into a roll. Before the car had stopped, it burst into flames. They never had a chance."

"Oh, Max, no! How horrible!"

"The neighbors had me stay with them awhile. They said I was too young to understand what had happened, too young to attend the funeral. So I never had the chance to say goodbye to my family.

"Of course they couldn't keep me indefinitely. They turned me over to the authorities and I was placed in a series of homes. I'm the first to admit that I was impossible. No one would have wanted to be around a kid acting the way I did."

"What did you do?"

"Anything I could to show my anger at the world, at the people around me, at myself for not having gone with my family that day. I was a destructive little beast, no denying that. I knew that I should have been with them. If I hadn't wanted to stay and play with my friends, I would have been there, too."

"But, Max! You would have been killed!"

"But I would have been with them." Once again she heard the small boy's lament as he said softly,

"They went off and left me all alone. They abandoned me. So I did everything I could to make those around me understand that nobody would ever hurt me like that again."

"Oh, Max." She wrapped her arms around him and hugged him, holding him even closer than before.

After a long silence he said, "By the time I was thirteen I was on the streets, tougher than the tough." She could feel him beginning to relax. "I look back now and wonder how I managed to survive. I ran with a gang that would give any mother nightmares."

"So how did the Max of the streets become the Max I know, fighting for truth and justice and the American way of life?"

He chuckled. "It wasn't an easy transition, let me tell you. I happened to pick the wrong guy to mess with one night. I thought he was an idiot to be out in our neighborhood alone past midnight, but I was cocky enough to figure that I could take him. He had me on my back in less than a minute with a raging headache and a broken wrist. That's how I met Johnny Davenport. He was a detective with the police department. After he half killed me he took me home with him, cleaned me up, took me to Emergency to have my wrist put in a cast, then demanded to know where my folks lived. Rather than book me, he was determined to take me home and make me face whatever I was running from. When he found out I didn't have anything to run from, he ended up taking me in to live with him and his wife. God, was he tough! I thought I was such a hard case. This man was something else. Of course he made up a bunch of rules that made me furious. I had to go back to school; I'd dropped out two years before. I had a curfew. I had to report everything I did. I thought I was in jail. But the thing was, I respected this guy. He was everything I was trying to be. So I stayed; I listened; I watched; and I learned. He sent me off to college. I couldn't believe it. He was willing to put his money into my education. Me, some punk kid who tried to steal from him.''

''Where is Johnny now?''

''He died during my senior year at college. I found out from Sarah, his wife, that he had discovered two months before he died that he had cancer. He didn't tell me, of course. That wasn't his way. He'd insisted that I live on campus, so I wasn't seeing much of him, although we talked on the phone fairly often. He left me a letter, telling me all the things he had never been able to say about his feelings for me. About how much I had contributed to the fulfillment of his life. How he expected me to go on and make something of myself, that I had to do it for me and that I had to do it for him, too. That he never backed losers and that he'd recognized a winner, even if I'd worn a powerful disguise.''

"He sounds like a wonderful man."

"Yeah. He was."

"What happened after college?"

"I was recruited by the government to work for them. I was ideal for the purpose. No family to worry, no problems with the law. As much of the punk stuff as I pulled, I'd managed to keep my record clean. Of course they had investigated me and knew about everything I'd ever done. Hell, they must have interviewed every person that had even a speaking acquaintance with me. I've never understood why they decided to hire me."

"Somehow that doesn't surprise me, Max. You don't seem to have a clue why anyone would want to get closer to you."

Once again he ran his hand up and down her spine. "Well, I have to admit that you're pretty damned close to me right now."

"And enjoying every minute of it!"

"You've gotta be kidding. I've bored you with the story of my life...." His voice trailed off with his words. "You know, I don't recall ever telling anyone about my life before. Johnny never asked; the Agency already knew. I've spent so many years putting it behind me that I haven't even thought about it."

"I'm glad you did. It helps me understand you better."

He kissed her... a slow, leisurely and very thorough kiss. And for the next few hours their conversation was the whispered murmurings of new lovers—exploring, sharing, expanding their knowledge of each other.

Lying now in Teresa's bedroom, Marisa stretched and turned one last time before falling asleep, a smile of contentment on her face.

Four

Max lay on the narrow bed in one of Teresa's upstairs bedrooms, unable to sleep. He had pounded and reshaped his pillow until the stuffing was in danger of falling out. He had kicked off his covers hours ago, allowing the slight breeze to brush over his overheated nude body.

All he could think about was his need for sleep. Hell, he hadn't had more than a couple of hours' sleep at a stretch since Marisa had called him...how many nights ago was that? Two? Three? It seemed more like a hundred nights. He needed some sleep, dammit. He didn't need to be lying there thinking about Marisa in the other bedroom across the hall. She sure as hell wasn't having any trouble sleeping.

He thought about their conversation in the garden. He didn't believe that she would have done anything different, regardless of what he had told her about his feelings for her.

Given what he'd learned about her the night they were almost killed, he understood why she had trouble accepting the idea that he would be the one giving her orders. He had managed to suppress the memories of that night for years—until Marisa's call. Now he couldn't get them out of his mind. With eyes closed, he began to live through the sequence of events once more....

Everything seemed to be going according to plan when suddenly he'd found himself surrounded. Three men were moving rapidly toward him. There was no way he could have handled three of them. The shot she had fired from somewhere near the bottom of the cliffs had caught them by surprise, and within minutes he had sprinted to her, breaking through the ambush that should have killed him.

By then the tide was coming in, effectively trapping them at the bottom of the cliffs. He'd been searching for a way up the sheer bluffs when he'd stumbled across the hidden entrance to the cave. He had hoped it would lead to an opening in the bluffs that would put them above the water mark that clearly showed along the top of the entrance. They didn't have much of a choice but to explore the cave and hope they'd find an escape route.

What he remembered most vividly was Marisa's willingness to follow him wherever he led. He'd never known a woman with so much courage.

He'd followed the narrow passageway, encouraged by the fresh air that swept through it. When they stepped out into the fairyland glow of the large cave, he felt as though he'd stepped onto the set of a Spielberg movie. Any minute a lake would appear with a pirate ship floating upon it.

The relief of recognizing that they had beat the odds, that they were safe, hit him so solidly he could scarcely stand. They'd made it, thanks to Marisa's quick thinking.

He remembered grabbing her, wanting her to know what he was feeling, but those feelings were all mixed up—fear, sexual desire, joy, a sense of deliverance. The overwhelming rush of emotions that he'd always been so careful to control swept over him.

By the time a bit of sanity had returned to him, it was too late. He'd blown his professionalism all to hell. He'd made love to her.

Even now he winced at the memories. What a stupid, stupid thing to do. He could rationalize all he wanted to, but the fact remained that he'd made a mess of things.

As if that weren't enough, he'd compounded his stupidity by pouring out all that garbage about his childhood. Why had he told her all of that?

As polite as she'd been, he knew she must have been bored.

But she had listened . . . and he'd felt a release that was as intense as any sexual release he'd ever experienced. He would never forget the hours afterward as long as he lived, when he had turned to her with conscious deliberation and showed her how much he loved her.

Once again he relived the sensations as though they were happening to him all over again.

Still curled beside him, she responded as though she knew just what he wanted and needed from her. Her skin felt like satin beneath his callused palms. He cupped her breast and slowly lowered his mouth until he could flick his tongue across an exquisite peak.

She moaned slightly, moving so that his mouth more fully covered her breast. Her restless hands explored and stroked his body until a fiery need engorged him. His need had been so great the first time that he had rushed their lovemaking. Despite the increasing urgency now, he continued to take his time, leisurely exploring her body with his mouth until she was quivering in his arms.

By the time he finally took her they were both past their limits of control. This time he set a strong, not frantic, pace . . . exhorting her to grab a handful of those stars they could see shining in the nighttime sky. He kept a tight rein on himself, determined to pleasure this woman as long as his endurance held.

When he finally reached his limit, he gave one final lunge and buried himself deep within her, holding her to him in a convulsive and primitive possession.

They had fallen asleep for a while. He didn't know what awakened him later...perhaps a shifting of the rocks around them, perhaps a trickle of pebbles and dirt from somewhere high above. He'd opened his eyes and looked around. The cavern still glowed like a fairyland. He glanced down at Marisa, curled in his arms.

He lay there watching her, thinking that she was the loveliest person he'd ever seen . . . knowing that he would love her until the day he died.

So what in the hell was he going to do about it? After all that maudlin talk of his past she was probably bored with him, although she certainly hadn't acted as though she were bored when he'd made love to her. He'd never made such tender love with anyone, or been treated so tenderly in return. It almost brought tears to his eyes, thinking about what had just happened between them. He felt whole . . . and renewed . . . as though he could have it all: a profession and a personal life. What kind of personal life would be up to Marisa, of course.

She stirred, her eyes fluttering open. When she saw that he was awake, she glanced around them with a quick scrutiny. "What's wrong?"

God, he felt good! "Nothing's wrong. Everything's right from where I'm looking." His gaze lovingly surveyed the diminutive length of her.

Her smile looked sleepy and very content.

"You know," he said in a tender voice, "I don't know much about you at all. Here I've been spilling my guts. What about you?"

She ran her hand across his chest. "What about me?"

"What made you get into this profession?"

"I suppose I wanted to learn how to protect myself, how to provide for myself, how to fulfill a vow I'd made when I was a little girl—never to have to rely on anyone but myself."

"Were you an only child?"

She shook her head. "I was the oldest of three girls."

"Where are your sisters now?"

She was quiet for a moment. "Julie lives in California. Eileen is in Seattle."

"What was your childhood like?"

She sighed. "Learning to be as unobtrusive as possible. Whenever my father drank, which was almost every day, he came home in an unpredictable mood. He had a terrible temper, and my sisters and I were scared to death of him. We never had a clue what would set him off, what we had done . . . or not done. As soon as we heard his pickup truck drive up, we'd run and hide.

"I remember one time when he was upset about something...I never did know what...and he hit my mother. She fell against the table and hit her head on the corner. Looking back now, I realize that he thought he'd killed her. I've never seen him so scared. I can't remember how old I was at the time . . . I was still in grade school . . . but I remember being so upset over my mother and embarrassed because the ambulance came and took them away, and everybody came running over to see what had happened. I didn't want anyone to know that he'd hurt her. So I made up a story about my mother being up on a chair trying to get something off a kitchen shelf. I said that she had fallen . . . and wasn't it wonderful that my dad had been there to take care of her." She shook her head. "I was always making up stories about my dad. I wrote glowing papers for school about what a great father he was and how he took us places and bought us things. I completely invented a mythical father."

"Did he behave differently toward everyone after your mom was hurt?"

"For a while. He used to come home much earlier, right after he got off work, rather than stop off at the bar for a few drinks. But he was just as irritable. Julie used to say that he was very even-tempered: he was mean all the time."

"Did your mother ever consider leaving him?"

She sighed. "The subject came up once as I was growing up. I had gotten a job working after school as soon as anyone would hire me. I saved and saved my money until I thought I had enough. Then I went home and gave it all to her and told her that now we could leave him and start over somewhere else. I'll never forget the look on her face. She was shocked at the suggestion. Absolutely stunned. She said that she loved him. That she would always love him. That she couldn't imagine life without him. I guess she was right. He was killed in a one-car accident when I was seventeen. He didn't make a curve, ran off the road and hit a tree. Mother died six months later. I always felt that she stopped living the day he died. It just took six months for her body to give up."

They were both quiet for several moments before Max asked, "What happened to you and your sisters after that?"

"Mom's oldest sister took us home with her. She lived about five hundred miles from our home, so we had to relocate. I didn't really care where we lived. I just wanted to get away from that town where everybody knew us, and everybody knew that my dad was drunk when he died."

"But you went on to college."

"Yes. My aunt and her husband offered to send us all to college. I refused their offer. From that point on, I was determined to do everything for myself. I never wanted to be dependent on anyone the way my mother was. Between working two jobs and a couple of scholarships, I managed to put myself through school."

"You'd just gotten out when you came to work for the Agency."

"That's right."

"You were carrying a pretty big chip on your shoulder, as I recall."

"At least with you, I was!"

"Why me?"

"Because I felt that you didn't think I could do my job, that someone else would have to cover for me."

"Instead, you covered for me tonight. I wouldn't be here, holding you in my arms, if you hadn't jumped into danger to save my neck."

She ran her hand along his thigh. "Not to mention other parts of your anatomy."

"You're a wanton woman, I must say...and I just want you to know how much I appreciate that aspect of your personality."

They both laughed and during the ensuing playfulness they managed to turn the fun to sheer sensual pleasure. The pleasure once again became fulfillment.

* * *

Reliving six-year-old memories wasn't helping him get to sleep, that was certain. Max got off the bed and walked to the window of Teresa's small bedroom. How the hell did he expect to sleep if he was going to dwell on memories like that! He reached for one of his cigars, which were lying on the small table near the bed, and put it to his mouth. After striking a match and touching the flame to the tip of the cigar, he drew on it until it glowed hotly in the dark.

They'd had one night together, not knowing what would greet them the following morning.

As soon as it was light enough to see if someone was waiting for them, they had carefully made their way back to the entrance of the cave. There was a broad expanse of sand awaiting them and no sign of their would-be assassins.

Eventually they had made their way to their hidden car and returned to their base. When Max had called the man whose position he had later assumed, he'd been told to abort the assignment and come home.

He wondered if she regretted telling him about her father. He had heard the pain in her voice and her determination not to be like her mother. She was certainly nothing like her mother. He couldn't imagine the Marisa he knew allowing anyone, male or female, to treat her harshly.

But he had realized that she was afraid of commitment and that he could scare her off very easily if he told her how serious he was about her. He was surprised himself. He would have to use caution and diplomacy and tact with her if he hoped to keep her in his life. She had left before he'd been able to talk to her.

The heat of the cigar against his fingertips brought Max to the present once more. Quickly he stubbed out the cigar and turned back to the bed.

He had to get some sleep. He was so tired that he could scarcely stand, and yet his mind refused to shut off.

What he needed was— Never mind what he needed. Never mind that she was a few feet away, just across the hall. Never mind that his body ached for her.

Never mind . . . never mind . . . never mind.

Five

They approached the small cove in silence, as the night spread its cloak of concealment around them. They had fallen into their working relationship with an ease that surprised Max, considering the length of time that had passed since they'd last worked together, as well as the tension that seemed to spring up between them at the least provocation.

He scanned the area for long minutes before signaling to Marisa to begin their descent to the water's edge. He had arranged to meet one of the small boats from the fishing trawler at midnight. They were only a few minutes early. He edged closer to the water and looked out to sea.

There was no sign of anything on the water. He motioned to Marisa to head for the deeper shadows that clung to the base of the steep incline. As they silently moved to that side of the cove, he saw what he'd been looking for.

A small boat waited in the shadows made by a clump of rocks near the water's edge. Max felt relief surge through him that they would be able to leave tonight.

After the previous night of restless sleep, then another day spent in Marisa's company, he was hanging on to his hard-won composure by a very thin thread.

They had bought her another change of clothing—black slacks with a black knit sweater. They'd covered her bright hair with a scarf.

He watched Marisa now as she acknowledged the two men waiting beside the boat. Following their mimed instructions, she scrambled inside as they pushed off from shore. Max waded out with the men until the water was deep enough for the three of them to get in without dragging the bottom of the boat against the shallow shoreline.

They kept their voices low in order not to attract any attention. He and Marisa had arrived at the rendezvous by taking a very roundabout route to make sure they weren't followed. They had seen no one on the way. He planned to keep it that way, if possible.

As soon as he was settled next to Marisa, she leaned over and whispered into his ear, "This really brings back memories of the times you and I worked together, doesn't it?"

He made a guttural sound in his throat and hoped she would accept it as his response. He didn't want to think about the fact that she was so close to him, not in his present mood and condition. He was a professional, dammit, and a good one. He'd spent the past six years reminding himself how fortunate he was that things had worked out as they had between them. He must have been temporarily insane to have considered the possibility of the two of them having a future together. He'd been caught up in all those fantasies of the moment, that's all. He should have left them behind in the fantasy cavern.

But he *was* human and he still found her extraordinarily attractive. Having her pressed tightly against his side at the moment did nothing to relieve the problem.

The two crewmen picked up their oars and began negotiating the waves back to the trawler while Max did his best to ignore the heat of her body against him.

He glanced around when he felt her move and watched as she leaned forward slightly so that her arm was free, then retied the large black scarf she wore over her hair. He found it irritating that he noticed every move she made, but he didn't seem to be able to ignore her.

As soon as they boarded the trawler the captain weighed anchor and started the engines. One of the men took them below, pointed to bunk beds, and then left them.

"Shall we flip a coin?" Marisa asked with a teasing smile.

He could have done without her cheerful acceptance of the primitive surroundings. He felt like the Grinch to her Mary Poppins. He turned away as he said, "Take whichever one you want. I don't care. I'll be on deck for a while."

"Max?"

He turned and looked at her. "Yes?"

"We make a good team. We'll get O'Donnell, and we'll find Timmy. Somehow I know we will."

Their eyes met and held. In this close area the tension between them was almost palpable.

He turned away once again. "Get some sleep. I'll be back down later."

Marisa watched him go before she turned to the bunk. She decided to sleep on top so that he could slip into bed later more easily. She sat down on the edge of the bunk and removed her shoes, then climbed up on the top bunk and stretched out.

She was tired but too keyed up to sleep. She lay there thinking about the past few days, thinking about Timmy. Had she guessed right? Did Troy have

the boy with him? If so, why would he use an innocent child in such a way? Was Timmy frightened?
She couldn't allow herself to think that way, or she'd
go mad.

She closed her eyes, determined to fall asleep.

It was several hours later when a sudden blast of
thunderous sound and a wild rocking threw Marisa
out of the bunk. She landed on the deck with a
thump. She felt as though she were in a nightmare,
but this was real. The rough surfaces around her
scraped her arms and legs, and pulled at her hair.

Gasping, she felt around in the dark, trying to
come to grips with what had just happened. There
must have been an explosion on board the trawler.
She could smell smoke but could see nothing in the
murky darkness.

Before she could fully draw breath she heard
Max's voice from somewhere nearby. "Marisa! Are
you all right? Where are you?"

"Here!" she managed to say, still without much
breath. The small space had a rakish tilt that she
found ominous. She felt his hand brush against her
face. She grabbed it and said, "We've got to get out
of here!"

She heard his chuckle, a sound she had never expected to hear from him again. And why now, for
God's sake!

"I always said you were quick in an emergency."

He was teasing her! Maybe she *was* dreaming, after all.

The trawler gave a shuddering groan just as Max tugged her toward what she presumed was the only escape.

"Watch the steps."

She used her other hand to reach out and try to identify her surroundings. Her toe hit the rung of the first step of the stairway. Max grabbed her waist and shoved her upward. She wasted no time scrambling to the top and glancing around. Controlled chaos was the best description of the scene. All the members of the crew were busy working on several small fires.

Max was beside her in seconds. "We've got to get off this thing before it blows sky high. C'mon." He knelt beside a metal bin and began to throw out life preservers and jackets. "Put on one of these," he ordered, following his own instructions.

One of the crewmen came up. "The captain suggests you take one of the boats, sir."

"What about the rest of you?"

"He hasn't given orders to abandon yet, sir."

Max shook his head, then gave the crewman a hand lowering the boat over the side.

The flames cast an orange-red glow on every surface. *This is what I always imagined hell would look like,* Marisa thought.

With the crew member's help they started to climb down to the boat. The waves were choppy, causing the boat to bounce around. Marisa gazed down at it in dread. It was bad enough trying to transfer to a smaller boat . . . a moving target was even scarier.

"Hurry!" Max ordered.

She closed her eyes and lowered herself down the short ladder, then opened them in time to spring into the boat, grabbing the gunwales and inching toward the bow, out of Max's way.

Later she was never sure what happened. One moment Max was balancing, ready to leap into the smaller boat, the next moment a large swell lifted the boat away so that when he jumped, Max was thrown against the gunwale, hitting his head.

"Max? Are you all right?"

She scrambled over to him, ignoring the fact that they were now drifting away from the damaged ship. "Max?"

He lay where he'd fallen. There was so little light. He was just a shadowy figure slumped in the middle of the small boat. She reached him and touched his face. He didn't stir.

"Oh, Max!" She felt along his cheek and discovered a large bump on his temple. Frantically, she looked around her, seeking help. They were continuing to drift farther and farther away from the burning ship.

The water looked black and oily in contrast to the bright flames emanating from the ship. She looked to see if there were other boats being lowered, but she could see nothing.

She felt around until her fingers touched a locker. Praying that she could find help, she lifted the lid. The first thing she touched was a flashlight, thank God! She turned the beam toward Max. He didn't respond to the light at all. She checked his pulse and was relieved to discover a steady beat, although too rapid to be normal.

The side of his face showed bruising and was beginning to swell.

She attempted to get in a more comfortable position, then pulled a blanket from the locker and covered him. She didn't know what else to do. The trawler had disappeared from view except for an occasional sighting when they topped a swell.

Why would a fishing boat suddenly go up like that, for no reason? Or were they, perhaps, the reason? She shivered. They could have been killed. Even now, drifting as they were, they could still die. What if Max didn't regain consciousness? She wouldn't allow herself to think about it. She had been in tough situations before; she'd been trained to keep her head in emergencies. Without his guidance, she would have to make the decisions on her own.

She heard an explosion and glanced back the way they had come. Flames shot into the sky and she knew the trawler was gone. She watched in silence until the sky was dark once more and prayed that the others had managed to escape.

She wondered what time it was. She had no way of knowing whether she had been asleep for hours or mere minutes before the explosion. There was no way to guess how long it would be before dawn.

She dug into the locker, examining their supplies. There was a canvas that could be used to shelter them from the sun, as well as packaged food and bottled water. There were also some flares.

Marisa lost track of time as she set off the flares, praying that someone would find them. Periodically, she checked on Max. He didn't stir.

Eventually her energy flagged and she fell asleep, Max's head cradled in her lap.

When the hail came, Marisa opened her eyes in confusion and glanced around. Early-morning sunlight surrounded them. But more important, there was a large yacht not far away with a smaller boat nearing them.

She glanced down at Max. Oh, dear God, but he looked bad. His coloring was gray, except for the brilliant hues on the side of his face.

"Max? Can you hear me? We've been spotted, Max. Help is on its way." She leaned down and laid her cheek against his. "Hang on, will you?"

She glanced up at the approaching cruiser. Whatever possible danger they might be in as a result of their rescue, it would be up to her to protect them. If the explosion had not been an accident, if someone was actively seeking survivors, then they were far from being out of danger.

But Max needed medical attention. It was up to her to do what had to be done.

Six

"Ahoy there, are you all right?" a voice hailed from across the water.

"Oh, Max," she whispered. "Here's hoping I handle this well enough to keep us both alive." Then she turned and waved to their rescuers. She leaned over Max, attempting to shield him from the bright sunlight while she checked his pulse. It had slowed to a more regular beat, which eased her fear.

The runabout came alongside of them. One of its occupants leaped to their smaller boat and attached it to the larger one, then waved for the other boat to head back to the yacht.

Marisa knew she had to come up with a story, right now, that would be plausible and still protect their identity. She remembered their last assignment and knew that their cover story then would have to do now.

She didn't have to fake her relief when she turned to the man in the boat with them and said, "I don't know how you spotted us, but I'm certainly thankful you did. My husband and I had to abandon our sailboat. He was knocked out just before we managed to get away." She turned back to Max and placed her hand on the undamaged side of his face. "I hope he's all right."

"Don't worry, ma'am. We'll be at the yacht in just a few minutes. There's a doctor on board."

That was certainly good news.

"I'm Marisa Chapman...and this is my husband, Max," she lied with a smile. "We've been vacationing here in the Mediterranean and having a wonderful time until last evening, when the boat we rented developed a mammoth leak and we had to abandon her." She rubbed her forehead. "It's going to be such a mess, trying to work out the damages and rental fees and all."

She hoped she sounded like a befuddled woman who couldn't function well without her mate. "Max always handles those things, you know," she added for good measure. Glancing down at him, she said, "I don't know what I'd do without him."

As soon as the words left her mouth she felt a flash of insight. She knew the truth of her words. She didn't know what she would do if she didn't know that Max was somewhere in the world, doing what he needed to do, being who he was.

She had run from that strength and sense of purpose. She'd felt threatened by it. And yet...now that he was helpless, she realized that she much preferred him the other way. She wanted to see him strong again, wanted to hear his brusque voice giving orders and impatiently waiting to see them carried out.

Somehow she had changed over the years. She wasn't as easily threatened by the men she met. She looked down at Max, seeing his vulnerability, and she wanted to protect him from all harm until he could regain consciousness and protect himself.

"Where are you people from?"

"Kansas City, Missouri. That's the Midwest, you know."

The man nodded. The Chapmans from Missouri, she reminded herself. She'd need to tell Max as soon as he came to.

By the time they reached the yacht Marisa realized she was shaking with nerves. She prayed that Max's injury wasn't too severe and that he'd regain consciousness before much longer.

As soon as they were on board, a distinguished-looking man wearing a swimsuit and shirt greeted them.

"Welcome aboard the *Tempest*. I'm George Olson, originally from San Diego, California," he offered with a grin, "but since retiring I haven't spent much time there."

He took her hand and shook it as the crew member who had been with her in the boat introduced them before helping the others to move Max.

Marisa watched them carry Max's limp body inside and turned to follow them.

George smiled and said, "I know how worried you must be. Let me show you to the guest room where you and your husband will stay until we can return you to shore." Obviously trying to allay some of her fears, he continued to talk as he held open a door for her. "Because of some medical problems I've been having, I have a highly skilled doctor on board. He's waiting below to examine both of you."

"Oh, I'm all right," she hastened to assure him. "Thirsty, perhaps."

Marisa glanced around the interior of the yacht. She had never seen such elegance. She followed their host through a magnificent stateroom and down a hallway. He paused beside an open doorway and motioned Marisa to precede him.

If this was a guest room, she wondered what the master suite looked like! She couldn't seem to take all of it in. What her mind and eyes focused on was the bed where Max lay. A man in a white shirt and shorts, who Marisa assumed was the doctor, examined him. He looked up when he heard Marisa.

"He's definitely suffering from a concussion. Do you have any idea how long he's been unconscious?"

"Since sometime last night. I don't know exactly when the accident happened." It didn't take much effort to sound worried and ineffectual. "I didn't know what to do. It was just awful." She stared at Max. "Is he going to be all right?"

"Head injuries are unpredictable. At this point all I can do is monitor him. We'll have to see how it goes. Has he regained consciousness at all?"

"No."

She turned away from the man, ashamed of the spurt of tears that suddenly filled her eyes.

George spoke in a kind voice. "I'll have the steward bring you something to eat, Mrs. Chapman. I know this has been difficult for you." She nodded without speaking. "Why don't you shower while I find some fresh clothes for you? My daughter has several things on board, although she's away at college at the moment. I'm sure she won't mind if you use some of her clothing and other items."

Marisa glanced down at her clothes and made a face. There was a tear in the knee of her pants, and a ragged patch on her shoulder where something must have snagged her sweater.

"Thank you. I really appreciate your help."

"No problem, no problem. I'm just glad we spotted you."

He turned and left the room. The doctor walked over to her. "I'd like to check you, as well," he said. She sat down docilely and allowed him to check her vital signs. When he was through, he nodded. "Nothing a little food and rest won't cure. You were both quite lucky, you know."

She remembered the sky lit up with flames and shuddered. "Yes, I know."

He patted her on the shoulder. "You'll feel better after a shower and some sleep."

She watched him leave the room, quietly closing the door behind him. She went over to the bed and sat down on its edge. "Oh, Max." She took his hand in hers. "Please be all right."

She sat there with him until the steward appeared with a tray and a small stack of clothing.

"Thank you," Marisa said, taking the clothing and watching him set the tray on a small table nearby.

She went into the bathroom and for the first time got a glimpse of herself. No wonder they thought she was in bad shape! Her hair stood out from her head as though she'd just been electrocuted. Her forehead, nose and cheeks were fiery red. The rest of her skin was so pale it looked almost green!

Turning away from the unsavory reflection, she stripped out of her clothes and crawled under the shower, feeling its warmth soothe and ease her tense muscles.

By the time she dried off, she felt much better. She looked through the clothing she'd been given and found underwear that was stretchy enough to fit. A pair of shorts and a sleeveless blouse completed her attire. She returned to the bedroom and ate the salad that had been left for her. By the time she finished, she could scarcely keep her eyes open. Stretching out beside Max, she fell asleep.

Where was he? Max blinked his eyes, trying to focus them. He had one hell of a headache—a world-class hangover—and he was having trouble with his vision. Finally, he realized that it was night. No wonder he couldn't see. He shifted slightly, trying to ease the ache in his head. A groan escaped him.

"Max?"

He heard the gentle whisper and turned his head.

"Oh, Max, you're awake. How are you feeling?"

He started to speak, and for the first time became aware that his mouth and throat were so dry that he could scarcely swallow. Anticipating his need, she reached for a glass nearby and handed it to him. He wet his lips and allowed the water to trickle down his throat.

"The doctor left some tablets for you, in case you needed them for pain."

"Doctor?"

"Oh, of course you don't realize where we are now."

"No," he admitted, accepting the tablets and swallowing them. He handed her the glass.

"Oh, Max, I was so worried. You hit your head when we were leaving the fishing trawler. Everything happened so fast. I wasn't able to signal to anyone that you were injured and we ended up drifting away from it. Thank God we were able to leave before that last explosion. I hope the others got away all right."

He thought about what she said for several moments, trying to assimilate it.

"The doctor said you must be quiet for the next few days. As it turns out, the man who owns this yacht was heading toward Monaco, so we won't be far from our original destination." When he didn't respond, she said, "I told them here on the yacht that we're on vacation and were on our way to Nice. I just hope this doesn't delay my catching up with Troy to see if he knows where Timmy is. Do you think you're going to be in good enough shape by the time we get there to face Harry O'Donnell? Should I send a coded message to your office requesting assistance?"

Max closed his eyes, too confused to follow her remarks. He would rest. Perhaps by morning he would be able to make some sense out of what she had said.

Marisa watched him for a long time. The tablets must have worked. He didn't stir for the rest of the night.

The next time Max awakened, the room was bright with sunlight. He was alone. With careful movements he climbed out of bed and made his way into the bathroom. When he washed his face he gazed into the mirror in perplexity. He obviously hadn't shaved in a few days. One side of his face looked puffy and was multicolored. He stared in silence at the image that looked back at him with a steady gaze.

His name was Max.

All the rest of the information the woman had given him the night before was jumbled in his mind. They were headed toward Monaco. They were trying to find someone by the name of Timmy. He was expecting to have a confrontation of sorts with a Harry O'Donnell. He was on vacation.

There had been something about a coded message. What had that meant?

Who was the woman who'd shared his bed last night?

The pounding in his head increased. He needed to lie down.

By the time he reached the bed, he felt exhausted. He lay down, closing his eyes. As he drifted off to sleep, he heard voices just outside the door.

"I'll check your husband, Marisa, just to confirm what you've already told us. I agree with you, though. Now that he's awake we can rest a little easier. I'm certainly glad to hear your news."

Too tired to attempt conversation, Max allowed his eyes to remain closed as he drifted toward oblivion once more.

Her name was Marisa. She was his wife.

The next day Max felt well enough to sit out on the deck with the others. He sat and watched and listened and waited.

He watched to see how each person in the party interacted with one another. Who felt what about whom.

He listened for information about the people, about their plans, about their lives.

He waited for his memory to return.

He didn't question that he had no intention of telling anyone that he couldn't remember anything. He merely followed his instincts. He was not going to give anyone the advantage of knowing how vulnerable he felt.

Not even Marisa. Not even his wife.

He watched her the most, trying to remember. Surely he would remember her, the woman he had chosen to marry.

His mind remained blank.

So he waited, he listened and he watched.

He also attempted to learn about himself. He had a very suspicious nature, he'd noticed. He didn't trust too many people. Of course he trusted Marisa, or at least he assumed he did. He just didn't want to give away any advantages that he might have.

He'd awakened from a dream in the middle of the night. He'd been making love to her.

Marisa.

His wife.

The dream didn't surprise him that much. He seemed aware of her no matter where they were, what they said, or what they did.

He noticed that she didn't touch him, which made him wonder about his constant need to touch her. Was it his present sense of isolation that made him want to reach out to her? Or was it the fact that they probably hadn't made love in a few days?

He had a hunch they had a very active love life. He'd certainly shown good taste in choosing her for a wife. Not only was she a dynamite-looking woman, she showed a high degree of intelligence and a very keen sense of humor.

He stood, uncomfortable with the strong bodily reaction he had every time his thoughts dwelled upon

Marisa. "I think I'll go inside. The sun's a little too bright for me."

"Are you feeling all right?" Marisa asked.

"Just tired. I may take a nap."

The doctor, who'd insisted they call him Henry, said, "Good idea. Give that head of yours a chance to heal."

Max wished to hell it would hurry. And by the way, how about returning his memory at the same time?

Once again his sleep was filled with dreams, or were they? Scenes appeared, then swirled away into the mist, only to be replaced by more and different scenes.

When he opened his eyes later, he felt more rested and more at peace. Things were coming back to him in fragmented pieces. He'd been in a classroom; later walking some cliffs with Marisa.

Invariably he was making love to her.

He got up and headed toward the bathroom. He had already stepped inside the small room when he discovered that Marisa was there. She'd obviously just turned off the water for the shower because she stood in the miniscule stall reaching for a towel.

"Oh!"

She was as exciting to see in the flesh as she'd been in his dreams. Why did he need to dream about her when she was there?

He picked up the towel and smiled at her. "Need some help?"

He was amused at her confusion. Why should she look so astonished at his suggestion? Surely it wasn't the first time he'd been with her in such an intimate situation. He took her hand and gently pulled her toward him, then carefully...and very thoroughly...dried her body.

Neither of them made a sound.

By the time he had completed his self-appointed task she was quivering, her eyes filled with the same need he was experiencing.

When their mouths touched at last, it felt like spontaneous combustion. He couldn't wait any longer. He needed her right now...at this moment. Without releasing her he slid his shorts off, the only item of apparel he wore at the moment, then lifted her, urging her legs around his waist.

She felt so damned good against his heated body. When she rubbed her breasts against his chest he wasn't certain he could hang on to his control and he groaned.

He'd intended to carry her to the bed, but he couldn't wait. Leaning her against the countertop, he eased himself inside her waiting warmth, grateful that she was obviously ready for him. Her response spoke volumes. She had needed him as much as he'd needed her.

It was over much too soon. He didn't want to release her. Not just yet. Placing her limp arms around his neck, he picked her up and carried her to the bed that he had left such a short time before.

He stretched out beside her, running his hands over her, reenacting all of his dreams about her.

"You're obviously feeling better," she managed to whisper, her breath coming in quick pants.

He grinned, feeling quite pleased with himself. "It would seem so." He leaned down and licked the pointed tip of her breast. Her body reacted as though she had received a sudden jolt of electricity. He settled against her to enjoy her response.

Eventually he began to explore, stringing a line of kisses downward, over her stomach, down her thigh to her knee, then returning along a path on her inner thigh until he paused, intimately touching her lightly with his tongue.

Once again her body jerked in response, her hands kneading his scalp and shoulders much like a kitten flexing its paws. He shifted and began to kiss her more fervently, holding her as she reacted to his intimate touch. He drove them both to a place of mindless overload of the senses before he relented and took her once more.

They shared touches and quick kisses while their bodies settled into a matched rhythm of offering, then releasing, giving, then withdrawing.

Max framed her face with his hands, holding her still so that he could enjoy each feature, each expression that flitted across her face. He whispered, "It's been so long." He felt safe in offering the comment. Even two days and nights was too long to wait for this.

He watched the myriad of expressions on her face at his words. Was he behaving differently than he usually did? Was it his fault that she hadn't been showing much affection toward him since he'd awakened to find himself without a memory?

Perhaps it *was* his fault that they had been so distant from each other. But he would make it up to her. He would show her how much he loved and desired her.

Such a task wouldn't create a hardship for him, regardless of his lack of memory of the past.

He could feel his body rejecting his conscious restraints, until he was forced to let go and allow his body its release. He felt her tightening around him, squeezing like a gentle vise until he cried out with the pleasure she was giving him. At his cry her body gave a convulsive surge, then began to pulse around him, drawing him closer and closer until they were no longer two distinct people, but one whole and perfect unit, complete in itself.

Max felt drained, the muscles in his body quivering at the release of tension. He turned so that he was stretched out beside her, both of his arms still around her.

She snuggled to him, drifting into sleep. He smiled to himself as he joined her.

Sometime later he awoke instantly when she began to stir.

"Where are you going?" he murmured, holding her against him.

"I think it's getting close to dinnertime. I thought I'd go shower and get dressed."

He heard a slight hesitancy in her voice and wondered at it. "Marisa, what's wrong?"

She pulled far enough away from him to see his face. After searching his expression, she shook her head a little, as though puzzled. "I'm just confused, that's all."

"About what?"

"You...me...us."

"What's so confusing about you...me...us?" he asked, deliberately mimicking her words.

"You've been so distant these past few days. And now—I guess I don't know what to think or how to act or—"

Knowing that they were on vacation, he was a little taken back by the fact that he had been distant.

"Oh, honey, I guess I've had so much on my mind that I didn't show you how I felt."

She eyed him uncertainly. "Max? Are you certain you're feeling all right?"

"I'm feeling better by the hour. Obviously, I was more than ready for a vacation."

"A vacation," she repeated carefully.

"So maybe this isn't like the one we planned, but we certainly can't complain about the luxuriousness of our surroundings. And George makes an admirable host. Once we get to Monaco we can—"

"Max?"

"What?"

"Do you know who I am?"

He smiled. "Of course I know who you are. You're Marisa."

Her relief was evident. "Do you remember why we're here on this yacht?"

"They rescued us. Why all these questions?"

"I don't know. I guess I'm just trying to figure out if that blow to the head created more of a problem than I first thought."

"Why? Because I wanted to make love to you?"

"Well, you have to admit your behavior is out of the ordinary."

He stroked over her sloping rib cage down to her narrow waist, then up over her hips, pausing at her thigh. It felt very natural, very normal to be lying here with her, touching her whenever and wherever he felt the urge. How could that possibly be out of the ordinary?

"You're acting as though we've never made love before."

"Well, it's been so long... I mean, we never really talked about what my leaving did to our relationship. I didn't know until I saw you again why you behaved the way you did. I got the impression that you no longer cared."

Ah, so that was it. The vacation was more in the form of a reconciliation. That explained a great deal to him. No doubt he was a proud man. As much as he might love her, having his wife walk out because of a fight wouldn't sit well.

"Well, I was hurt, of course. I mean, we belong together, and for you just to walk out like that, without giving us a chance to work things out, made me angry."

She was quiet, obviously considering what he had said. "You're right, of course. I was a coward to leave the way I did. But your promotion seemed to have changed so much for us. It was one thing to work as equals, but when you became my boss I was afraid that you would use your new power over me, not only as a boss, but as the man I loved."

She had admitted it! he thought with obvious relief. She loved him. Well, of course he had known that on some level by the way she had responded so wholeheartedly to his lovemaking. But for her to come right out and say so made a tremendous difference to him.

Knowing that she had left him had hit a nerve inside of him. He didn't like being left. He wasn't sure how he knew that, he just knew that it was true.

"Well, at least we're together now."

She sighed. "Oh, yes, we're together now. And we're safe . . . at least until we get to shore."

Safe? An alarm went off in his head. Hadn't they been safe before? Well, obviously there had been some sort of mishap at sea. Perhaps that was all she was referring to. But just in case, he would need to stay vigilant to the nuances around him.

She leaned over and gave him a quick kiss. "Let's go shower together. We'll save some time so we won't be late for dinner."

On the contrary—because they decided to shower together, they were very late for dinner!

Seven

"Do you like to fish, Max?" George asked at dinner that night.

Without hesitation, Max replied, "No, George, I don't." Then he wondered how he was so certain. He glanced at Marisa who was staring at him in surprise, her fork halfway to her mouth. *Oh hell, don't tell me I've been spending every weekend of our marriage fishing!*

"I don't suppose there's too many places to fish around Kansas City," George offered with a smile.

Max had a sudden flash of another place and time, of going out in a boat along the seashore. Kansas City? But hadn't he come from California? How did he know that? Even so, maybe he'd moved as a kid. But Kansas City? He drew a blank.

When Max didn't say anything, George said, "If you two aren't in any hurry, I thought we might spend tomorrow in an area where I like to do some fishing. Of course if you need to get to shore right away..." He allowed his words to trail away.

Once again Max glanced at Marisa. She was watching him intently. Perhaps she was wondering if he would insist that they leave the yacht as soon as possible.

But a vacation was a vacation, wasn't it? George was a hospitable host. At the moment he didn't care what he did for a living. No doubt there were people covering for him while he was on vacation.

He smiled at George. "We're in no hurry," he said, and reached for Marisa's hand. "Are we, darling?"

He noted that she quickly masked her surprise at his response but could not control the quiver of her hand in his. So she wasn't as sure of him and their relationship as she'd pretended. It was going to take some time to convince her, that was for sure, but he had to admit he was looking forward to it.

Later, while he stretched out on the bed and watched her getting ready to join him, Marisa said, "I was surprised to hear you say you didn't like to fish."

"Were you?"

"But then, maybe it isn't so surprising. You always went fishing with your dad. Your feelings about that time of your life must be all mixed up with the activities you shared with him."

He shrugged. "I guess I never gave it much thought."

"I also thought you considered our getting to Nice urgent."

He smiled. "Nothing seems as urgent to me as being with you. I feel as though I woke up to a whole new life the other morning. I want to savor it."

She rose from the small dressing table and came to him. "Oh, Max, do you feel that way, too? I feel as though we've been given a second chance to work things out between us."

He pulled her down beside him. "I feel the same way," he said with a grin, sliding the borrowed robe off her shoulders and revealing her fully to his view.

"Do you think you should contact your office? It wouldn't hurt to let someone know what's happened to you."

Call his office on his vacation? What sort of workaholic tendencies had he developed?

He kissed her below her ear and along her jawline. "If you really think I should call, I will... tomorrow."

Maybe by tomorrow he'd remember a little more about his life. In the meantime, he was going to enjoy each and every moment of today.

* * *

After breakfast the next morning, Marisa drew
Max aside and said, "I decided to call your office for
you this morning since you had slept in. I thought
your boss would accept my explanation that you
were fine, but after I told him you'd been hurt, he
insisted that you call him. He even gave me a more
direct number to call than the one I knew." She
handed him the slip of paper and Max frowned at it.

His memory was improving, just as he'd hoped.
Unfortunately, not so he could make any sense out
of what he remembered. He kept seeing things as
though he were a child. There were many scenes
where he felt desolation and despair. He wondered
why. What had gone wrong in his early life that the
few memories surfacing would make him feel so
much pain?

He was seriously thinking about telling Marisa
about his memory loss, but he hesitated to do so.
Would she be upset that he hadn't told her from the
very beginning? How would she react to the fact that
he had no memory of her before they boarded the
ship? Would she feel that he had taken advantage of
the present situation? As far as he knew, they had
just met. He didn't remember a thing about their
marriage. Nothing at all.

He wouldn't blame her if she were to be upset.
And what purpose would it serve, anyway, for him

to tell her? And yet it would be a relief to be able to discuss the matter with someone.

He glanced down at the piece of paper he was holding. Maybe he had found the answer for the moment.

Using George's state-of-the-art phone system, Max soon heard the ringing of the phone on the other end of the line.

"H'lo?"

"This is Max. Marisa said you wanted to speak to me."

"Yes. She said that you received a blow to the head and were suffering from a concussion, but that you seemed to be fine now. I wanted to make certain you were capable of handling Harry on your own. Otherwise I can have assistance waiting for you when you arrive in Nice."

Obviously he wasn't going to be able to handle Harry if he didn't know who the hell he was. Why jeopardize his job for the sake of secrecy?

"Actually, I do have something of a problem. I believe it will take care of itself as I grow stronger, but at this point I'm a little hampered."

"What's wrong?"

"It's a little complicated. The thing is, I, uh, don't remember anything."

"You what?"

"I've got some form of amnesia. I mean, it's not so severe that I don't know how to function or anything. It's as though everything prior to waking up with a god-awful headache was wiped from my mind."

"Max, this isn't something to be taken lightly. Why didn't Marisa mention it when she called?"

"She doesn't know. I haven't told anyone, including the doctor."

"How is that possible? If you don't remember anything how did you know to call me?"

"Marisa mentioned it. She was obliging enough to give me a new number, as well."

"So in your own inimitable fashion, you've been feeling your way along without any help and without giving anything away."

"Are you saying my behavior is typical, then?"

"Unfortunately, yes, it is. You never give away an advantage, no matter how small. I don't suppose she told you who I am?"

"No. Just that I work for you."

"That's true. Now listen to me. I don't want you attempting to play hero. As soon as you get to shore, take the next plane back to the States. We'll have you see a specialist. Forget O'Donnell for now. He can wait. Now that we know the truth about him, we can take care of him soon enough."

"Would you just answer one question? Exactly what sort of business are we in?"

There was a long silence. "I'm afraid I'm not at liberty to discuss the matter at the moment."

"Does our business have anything to do with my being in Europe on a yacht owned by George Olson?"

"Not directly, no. But you're safe enough there. I had him checked out thoroughly. He's who he says he is."

"What's all this business about being safe? Marisa mentioned it last night. I didn't want to question her too much."

"Marisa can answer your questions, Max. I'm curious why you've chosen not to tell her about your problem."

"I'm not certain. I just don't feel right about doing so."

"I've always trusted your instincts, Max, and I will continue to do so, regardless of the fact that you don't remember anything. Get back to the States as soon as possible. Perhaps your memory will start coming back by then. If not, we'll be able to get you the help you need."

"You're probably right. I keep getting flashes of scenes, but at the moment they don't mean anything to me. By the way, where are you?"

"Washington, D.C."

"Then why does everyone on board think we're from Kansas City?"

"Maybe that's one of the covers you and Marisa used in the past."

Covers? What was he talking about? "I'm afraid I don't follow you."

"Sorry. I can't go into any details at the moment. We'll talk again when you return."

Max hung up the phone and left George's office, his head pounding. He would go lie down for a while and see if that helped. Otherwise he'd get some pain tablets from Henry.

The pain was almost blinding. He felt his way down the corridors to their room, then let himself inside with a sense of relief.

He stretched out on the bed and took several deep breaths, trying to make his mind blank. Just as he began to drift away he remembered a question he'd meant to ask.

How long had he been married?

A slight noise at the door brought him abruptly awake sometime later. He was reaching under the pillow for his pistol when he realized that it was Marisa coming in.

His pistol? Why would he keep a pistol under his pillow?

"Oh, did I wake you?" she asked. "I'm sorry. I thought you were going to join me on deck when you got through with your call."

He allowed himself to relax back on the pillow. His head had eased somewhat, for which he was thankful. He wanted to avoid taking the pain tablets, if possible. They dulled his senses too much. He needed to stay alert.

Where had *that* thought come from?

"Marisa, we need to talk." He sat up on the side of the bed.

She sank down into a chair nearby. "What's happened? Has he heard from O'Donnell?"

"O'Donnell?"

She frowned. "Isn't that what we need to talk about? My trying to locate Troy and your neutralizing O'Donnell?"

He shook his head as though trying to break something loose that had become stuck. "I've got a slight problem, and you might as well know about it."

She leaned forward. "Okay."

"That blow to the head has left me a little confused. There are some memory lapses and I'm having trouble putting things together."

"Why haven't you mentioned it before?"

"I thought everything would come back to me without my having to say anything. I mean, it isn't as though I've forgotten *everything*." He attempted a laugh that sounded a little ragged. "I mean, I didn't forget how I feel about you."

She studied him for a moment. "Are you certain? A memory loss would explain some of your behavior these past few days."

"I'm fine, really. I didn't want you worrying about me."

She slowly settled back into her chair. "You know, I've enjoyed the way you've been the last few days, I must admit. It brought back some of the happier times we had together."

"I've enjoyed it, too."

"You've been so much more relaxed and open toward me."

"Have I?"

She grinned. "Mm-hm."

When she looked at him like that, every thought he'd managed to gather fled his mind. He reached for her and she willingly allowed him to pull her over until they were both sprawled sideways across the bed.

"More relaxed, you say?" He took her hand and placed it on a part of his anatomy that was far from relaxed.

She chuckled. "I had no idea I had such an instantaneous effect on you."

"Then I must be one hell of an actor. I react to you every time I see you . . . in the shower . . . in my bed . . . over breakfast . . . while you're soaking up the sun . . . I have a great deal of difficulty keeping my hands off you." All the time he was talking, his hands were rapidly removing her clothes.

She followed his lead, until they were lying there with nothing between them but the sea air wafting through one of the portholes.

This time Marisa became more assertive, shifting so that she was over him, her hands framing his face. "Let me make love to you, all right?" she whispered, placing feathery kisses over his face.

Max felt her breasts brush against him, her hair tickle his shoulder, then felt the movement of her hips, hands and hair touching, exploring and brushing against him. By the time her mouth had touched him intimately he was having trouble getting enough air in his lungs.

Enough! He couldn't take any more of this without exploding! He hauled her across him, lifting her so that she was sitting with her knees on either side of his thighs. He placed his hands at her waist and slowly positioned her until she took his hard length deep within her. She gave a quick sigh of delight just as he pulled her forward enough to taste one of the delectable breasts placed so conveniently before him.

He allowed her to control their pace, taking delight in her responses to what he continued to do with his mouth and hands. How he loved this woman! She was everything he could possibly want in a wife. Thank God he'd realized that sometime in his misty, forgotten past.

When he'd reached the end of his control he took over by once again holding her lightly between his hands and guiding her movements to meet his stronger, faster ones. She rode him well, her mouth seeking his as they were flung across the finish line in a burst of motion.

She collapsed across him, holding him tightly. He could feel her rapid heartbeat throbbing against his chest, hear her panting breaths trying to fill her lungs once more. The scent of her floral perfume wafted between and around them. Her taste was still on his lips. He slowly ran his tongue across them to enhance the moment.

When she raised her head what seemed to be a long time later, she was frowning slightly. "Max?"

"Hmm?"

"Maybe we shouldn't have been quite so energetic. Is your head all right?"

"Who cares? The rest of me is doing just fine, thank you."

"But I'm worried about you."

"The doctor said I'd have some residual pain and soreness. I'll be okay."

"No. I mean about your memory loss."

"Oh, that."

She slipped to his side and propped her head on her hand. "Yes, that." She poked him in the stomach lightly with her index finger. As though caught up in the experience of touching him, she ran her fingernail into the downy hair that grew on his chest and drew circles, watching as a path opened, then closed around the tip of her finger.

"Max."

"Mmm?"

"What do you remember about O'Donnell?"

"Not much," he admitted.

"Not that he's a traitor and may have been responsible for some of your men being killed?"

He forced himself not to physically react to her words as his mind raced at the implications of what she'd just said. His men? Killed? A traitor?

Whatever his occupation, it was dangerous. He knew that he worked out of Washington, D.C. A horrifying thought occurred to him. What if he was a gang lord? No! He wouldn't be. He couldn't be. Not and have such a strong negative reaction to the idea.

"Tell me about O'Donnell."

"Do you remember that I heard him planning to take care of somebody? He may be involved in the missing artifacts and other smuggling that's been going on."

"But we don't know?"

"No. You were going to get me out of the area first. I was going to continue to look for Timmy." She paused. "You remember Timmy?" He shook his head. "Timmy's my nephew. My sister's husband may have taken him."

"You were looking for him?" he asked, horrified at the thought that his wife would be doing something so dangerous.

"I was the only one she knew to ask," she said. Max heard the slight defensiveness in her tone and wondered if this is what they had argued about.

He wouldn't be at all surprised. All of it fitted. She had told him she was going to look for Timmy. He had told her not to, but she had, anyway. He'd followed her, obviously in time to get her away from this O'Donnell character.

Well, he'd certainly picked an independent one, he'd give her that. Obviously, she believed in doing what had to be done regardless of the consequences.

He admired her for that...in a way. He'd just have to learn to handle her with a little more finesse. Or maybe he'd learned his lesson. It sounded as though he was a real workaholic. Probably didn't spend enough time at home.

Maybe he'd needed that crack on the head! At least it seemed to wake him up!

Eight

——

The pain! Oh, God, but the pain made him feel as though his head was shattering. He fought his way out of a deep sleep, trying to understand why he hurt so badly. What was wrong with him?

He forced himself to sit up on the side of the bed. He'd been working too hard, that's all. He'd been so worried about— There was something that he'd been so worried about. What was it?

Something wrong in the field, that was it! He was losing agents and didn't know why. His head was pounding so hard that he could scarcely think. Maybe if he could take something for it. He reached for the lamp beside his bed but couldn't find it. He was more tired than he thought.

He got up and eased around the bed. He'd catch the hall light, which would give him enough illumination to find the kitchen. Every step was—

"Max? Is something wrong?"

He whirled around in surprise. There was a woman in his bedroom! Who in the hell—

A light came on, flooding the room with a brilliance that seemed to blind him.

"Max? What's the matter? Where are you going?"

That voice! He knew that voice. This wasn't the first time it had haunted him.

The room began to whirl around and around, shadows blending with the brilliant light...shadows and light...darker and darker...shadows and a slowly...dimming...light.

He felt himself falling and he sighed with relief. At last he was escaping from the pain.

"As I explained to you earlier, Marisa, head injuries can be very mysterious. I don't have any explanation for this latest development. I don't believe he reinjured himself when he fell. Luckily he was close enough to the bed that most of his weight fell across it. I can't explain why he has been unconscious for the past two days. I wish I could. The swelling around his temple has gone down; his pupils are back to normal. It's a mystery.''

Max lay there quietly, his eyes still closed, and listened. He was aware of a clarity of thought that had often eluded him in the past. It was as though he was standing at a point and could look back and see forever, then look forward and see equally well.

He'd been injured. But he was all right now. He remembered being thrown off balance as he left the trawler. He remembered falling and pain exploding in his head.

He remembered—he flinched from the memory. He was with Marisa. Somehow he had been convinced that they were married. How could he have believed that? How could his mind have tricked him in such a way? Was there part of him that had secretly wished it to be so?

He heard the door close softly across the room. Slowly he opened his eyes. The first thing he saw was Marisa leaning against the door, her hands covering her face.

''Marisa?'' he managed to say.

She jerked up her head and their eyes met. Hers were filled with tears. ''Oh, Max! I thought you were dying.''

She ran across the room and knelt beside the bed. ''I couldn't bear losing you again. It was bad enough the first time. I couldn't go through it again!''

What had he done? These past few days had been a fantasy he had played out, a chance to pretend that he had a loving wife, to pretend that he was a married man. He refused to make allowances for the fact that he had lost his memory. He knew that her pretending had been done as protection for them. She had used the same cover they had used during their last assignment. They had played a married couple on vacation. It was a good one that worked for them.

Unfortunately he had been one of those fooled this time.

The question was, what to do now?

"Marisa, I'm sorry."

She took his hand and held it between both of hers. "Please don't apologize, Max. The doctor said these things happen sometimes. How does your head feel?"

He thought about that for a moment and realized that he no longer had a headache. "It feels fine," he said, smiling. "Are you okay?" he asked, touching her cheek with his finger.

She gave a teary chuckle. "Much more than okay, now that you're awake once again." She gave him a mock stern look. "And I don't care how insistent you become, there's going to be no more lovemaking until we're absolutely sure that the activity didn't cause you to relapse!"

That was something, anyway. How could he deal with his tumultuous emotions if he continued to make love to her? Never had he felt such a confusion. He felt as though he'd just awakened from a dream—a wonderful fantasy of a dream—only to find that it had actually happened.

Despite all of his intentions, he had managed to get involved with Marisa once more, only this time she had made it clear that she wanted to work on their relationship.

How could he admit to her that he hadn't a clue how to go about doing such a thing? He'd gotten one thing right. He was a workaholic. His work was what he did best; what he felt most comfortable doing. He didn't have a very good track record with relationships. All of the people who had meant something to him—his parents, his sister, even Johnny, had all died.

Was what he felt for Marisa love? He didn't have a clue. Was he ready to make a commitment to work on a relationship? Two weeks ago—even one week ago—he would have said no.

Now he wasn't sure what to do. He felt as though he'd just stepped off a cliff and was hanging in air with nothing to support him. None of his past decisions could help him now.

Marisa came to her feet. "Let me go tell Henry the good news. I'm sure he's going to want to check you once again."

Damn, but he was tired of being poked and prodded. He wanted to get back to work. He had a job to do. That was the important thing to remember. He had a job to do.

"When do we arrive in Monaco?"

"George thinks we should be there when we wake up in the morning." She gave him a teasing smile. "I thought you weren't in a hurry to get there."

He closed his eyes. What could he say to her that wouldn't seem out of character? Or at least out of character for the loving man he'd pretended to be?

Pretended? Was that what he had done? Or was that loving man actually a part of him, buried deep inside his psyche, wanting to surface?

"I'd feel better getting the situation with O'Donnell cleared up, that's all."

"So would I, especially if Troy is involved. I wish I could understand why he would take Timmy like that. It never made sense."

"To spite your sister, didn't you say?"

She glanced at him, then away. "I suppose." She patted his hand. "I'll go get Henry. You lie still and rest."

When she left the room Max slowly sat up. The dizziness he'd felt earlier was gone. He touched his temple lightly. It was a little sore, but not much.

He'd been in tough situations before. Now he was going to have to deal with this one.

* * *

"I can't thank you enough for all of your help, George," Max said the next morning as they prepared to leave the yacht.

"Henry did the work, Max. I'm just glad we spotted you when we did."

"Yes, it could cause a man to consider the possibility of miracles, couldn't it?"

They eventually took their leave of their genial host and climbed into the cruiser for the trip to shore. The harbor was filled with vessels of all sorts arriving and departing. Max sat beside Marisa and watched the activity with a keen eye.

"There's something different about you," she finally said to him.

He turned his head and looked at her. "You're probably missing my Technicolor face. It looks rather bland these days."

"It's not that, Max. You just seem more aloof, somehow."

"I've been thinking about what we're going to do once we get to shore."

"That's it! You're no longer treating our time together as a vacation. You're back to work now."

"I suppose that's true."

"I miss the man on vacation."

He gave her a half smile. "I'm not even sure he exists."

"I know. It was a real shock for me, too, but a very pleasant one. I suppose it was finding out that you *do* love me that made such a difference. Where there is love anything can happen, even miracles."

He thought about her remark for the rest of the ride. *Where there is love.* Is that what made the difference? He did have a sense of no longer being alone in the world.

He rather liked the idea now that he was becoming adjusted to it.

As soon as they reached the quay, the crew members assisted them off the cruiser and waved goodbye. Marisa looked toward the streets. "Now what?"

"I need to make a phone call. Let's find a phone."

They walked several blocks before they found a public telephone. Within minutes Max was waiting for a distant phone to be answered. When it was, he said, "This is Max."

"I have your transportation arranged."

"There's no need. I'm all right now."

"Meaning?"

"My memory is back. My headache is gone. A few days' rest was all I needed."

"You're the best judge of your condition."

"Yes. Has there been any update on O'Donnell?"

"He reported in on schedule. Gave us information that would make certain that any men we send out would be in the interior for the next few days."

"So there's a good chance there will be a delivery made along the coast soon."

"That's what I concluded."

"Do you have men covering him?"

"Nothing so conspicuous. He would recognize them. I'm counting on the fact that he doesn't know we're on to him."

"But he saw Marisa."

"Does he have any reason to believe she'd report him?"

"Not particularly. He's aware that she left the Agency soon after I was promoted."

"Which might lead him to suspect that there's no love lost between you."

Interesting choice of words, Max decided.

"I'm going to try to send Marisa back to the States. However, I don't have any authority to force her to go and she insists that she wants to stay."

"Is there a problem with that?"

"You know the policy. She no longer has security clearance."

"Under the circumstances, I would suggest we bend the rules. If it weren't for Marisa, you'd still be working blind regarding the leaks in our system."

Max knew when he was licked.

"I'll call after I've made contact."

"You do that" was the dry response.

He hung up and turned to Marisa. "We need to rent a car and buy a map of the area."

"We? Does that mean you're no longer going to argue about the fact that I want to go with you?"

"Would it do any good?"

"No."

"Then I'll save my energy. Let's go."

They were within half a block of the car rental place when a black limousine silently drew up beside them. Out of habit long ingrained, Max grasped Marisa's arm and moved away from the car. But he was too late.

"Just get in the car and the lady won't get hurt," he heard as he was shoved into the back seat of the limousine by two men with handguns. Marisa stumbled in behind him. The automobile shot away from the curb and headed for open country.

Max cursed under his breath. He'd been behind a desk for too damned long. He should never have let this happen.

Marisa was already righting herself and peering around the car. The window between the driver and the back seat was up. They could not identify the driver.

"What do you suppose this is all about?" she asked in a low tone.

"I think O'Donnell has known where we were all along," he replied.

"Was he behind the explosion on the trawler?"

"I wouldn't be at all surprised."

"Then how does he know we survived?"

"He's one of the best in the business. He may have had contacts all along the coast watching for us. We weren't exactly inconspicuous this morning coming off that yacht."

"What are we going to do?"

"Wait until we see what we're confronted with."

Max watched for landmarks, tried to spot familiar terrain, but it was difficult since he hadn't been in Europe for several years.

He settled back and waited for the next scene to begin.

After more than two hours the limousine pulled between two stone pillars and followed a long, winding drive toward a weathered chateau. Nothing looked familiar.

As soon as the car stopped, the back door nearest Max opened. He stepped out, then turned and assisted Marisa. The man who had opened the door motioned for them to climb the steps to the front door. Before they reached the top, the door opened. A middle-aged woman in a domestic's uniform nodded and led them into a large room.

"M'sieur will be here shortly," she intoned, then turned and left.

Although the home itself was old, it had obviously been renovated and the furnishings were quietly luxurious. The paintings were the kind seldom seen outside of museums. When Max heard the door open behind him, he turned.

A man he'd never seen before walked into the room and strode to Marisa.

"Thank you, my dear. You did exactly as I suspected you would. Harry will be pleased."

Max heard her gasp the name "Troy!" So this was the man married to Marisa's sister.

In his late forties, he was slim with a debonair demeanor that Max assumed would be pleasing to most women.

"Do you know where Timmy is? Did you take him? I've been looking all over for you—"

"Yes, I know, my dear. And I had to lead you on quite a chase until you decided to get some help." He turned and walked over to Max. "I don't believe we've met, although I've certainly heard a great deal about you. My name is Troy Chasen and you must be the famous Max Moran."

Max gave him a straight look, then lifted his brow. "I'm not certain what I'm supposed to be famous for. Would you care to clarify that statement?"

"Ah, Harry didn't mention your modesty... another admirable virtue."

"Troy," Marisa said, joining them beside one of the Old Masters' paintings. "What is this all about?"

"It's really very simple, my dear, and really ingenious on my part, I must admit. Harry has been complaining about his employer's irritating habit of ruining many of our shipments of the past few years. He—or actually, we—decided to get rid of the troublesome fly in our ointment. The problem was how to coax him into our web. It was only a fortuitous accident that Harry discovered that my sister-in-law was Marisa Stevens, a former agent with whom he had worked. That's when I knew exactly what I needed to do to get our friend here to visit us.''

Marisa gasped and Max looked at her. She'd turned ashen as she stared at Chasen in horror. ''Oh, no, Troy!''

''That's right. I've always known your little secret, my dear. I just didn't realize who Max really was until recently. It was easy enough to check out the details, as well as the timing. Put that together with the various comments Eileen has made over the years and it was easy enough for me to draw an accurate conclusion.''

''I haven't the foggiest idea what you're talking about, Chasen,'' Max said. ''Just what in hell are you threatening her with?''

''Threatening? Why, nothing. What I counted on and what Marisa was predictable enough to do has delivered you into our hands, Max. Threatened with the loss of her son, Marisa immediately went to his father for help.''

Nine

"Where is Timmy, Troy?" Marisa demanded.

Max stared at the two of them, trying to make sense out of a senseless remark. Was the man deranged? What was he talking about? Marisa had mentioned that Troy wasn't the father of Eileen's son—Marisa's nephew.

"He's safe, Marisa. For the moment."

"How could you have done this, Troy? He's just an innocent child. You were always so good with him. Why would you put us both through such horror?"

"Necessity, my dear. Nothing more or less. We decided that Timmy would be the perfect lure to get

Max over here, away from his protected environment.''

''But he doesn't know,'' she cried. ''Don't you understand? He never knew!''

Max had once noted, quite objectively, that in periods of high stress, most particularly in life-threatening circumstances, time seemed to slow down, as though to give a person the opportunity to take in every action around him, analyze it and act in order to protect himself. This strange phenomenon had served him well at different times during his career. This time, he could think of nothing to protect him from the knowledge he'd just received.

The actual force of the blow when it finally struck him was so strong that he felt himself stagger for a moment. Both Marisa and Chasen were watching him intently. Marisa registered distress. Chasen registered detached amusement.

Anger surged through him as he began to put all the pieces together. Everything had been planned, right down to her phone call asking for help. Somehow they had known that he would run to her side.

No! That wasn't what Chasen was saying. They thought he knew about the boy. They thought the boy would be the lure to get him over there, the boy he'd never known existed.

''So now that you have me, what do you intend to do with me?''

"Ah, yes. Get to the bottom line, is it? Harry always said you never wasted time with extraneous details. He seems to know you well."

"Cut the crap, Chasen. What do you want with me?"

"I want you to get out of our affairs. My part of the bargain was to produce you. It's now up to Harry to dispose of you."

"Where's Harry?"

"Unavoidably detained, I'm afraid. Unfortunately, we weren't able to guess exactly where you might surface along the coast, so we were prepared for several eventualities. Therefore, his absence couldn't be helped. We do have a nice room where the two of you can spend your time waiting for him. He should be here by morning."

"I want to see Timmy," Marisa demanded.

"I'm afraid that's not possible. It wouldn't do the child any good to see you so upset, anyway. But don't worry, Eileen and I will be wonderful adoptive parents. He's already used to us, spends as much time with us as he does with you. Of course he'll be sad to hear that his mother was killed in an unfortunate accident while abroad, but he's young. He'll get over it."

Chasen nodded his head and two burly men stepped into the room. "These gentlemen will show you to your room."

Neither Max nor Marisa spoke as they followed one of the men up a winding staircase and down a long, well-lit hallway. Max glanced over his shoulder and wasn't surprised to see that the second man had followed them.

The first man opened a door and waved them through. As soon as they walked past him, he shut and locked the door.

Max immediately went over to the windows and discovered that they were barred. In less than five minutes he'd checked to see if there was another way out.

There wasn't.

Only then did he turn and look at the white-faced woman who sat in a straight-backed chair by an empty fireplace.

"Care to fill me in on the missing pieces?" he asked in a low voice.

Marisa turned and looked at him, her eyes filled with agony. "I fully intended to tell you, Max. When I realized how you felt about me I knew I'd made a dreadful mistake by not contacting you when I first found out I was pregnant. But I didn't know. I just didn't know."

"When, exactly, did you intend to tell me? I have a son... five years old, didn't you say... and I have to hear about it from some slimeball who's nonchalantly plotting to have me killed, and you reassure me that you intended to tell me? When?"

"I started to tell you when we were working in Teresa's garden, but I couldn't figure out a way to explain, since I'd already called Timmy my nephew."

"Does he know who his father is?"

She shook her head.

"Then how the hell did you explain his birth? Even five-year-olds are rejecting the stork story and the cabbage leaf theory."

"Max, please, I—"

"Max, please? Please, what? Please don't be angry? Please understand? Is this where you're going to tell me about how wonderful love is? How you kept the news that I had a son from me out of love?"

She came out of her chair. "Yes! Yes, I did. The man I made love to the night in the cave, the man with whom I made that beautiful baby boy ceased to exist once we returned to Washington. You became cold and autocratic, not the warm and tender man I thought I'd gotten to know."

"Well, for your information, cold and autocratic men have just as much right to be told they're going to become fathers as warm and tender ones have!"

"I know that! I'm not trying to excuse what I did. There's no excuse."

"I'm glad we've found something we can agree on."

They stood facing each other like two boxers in a ring, their bodies tense, their anger palpable.

"I had no idea I was pregnant when I resigned. I'd been at my sister's almost two months before it occurred to me that something was wrong. At first I thought it was because I was so upset. I'd quit the profession I enjoyed, moved across the continent from the man I loved—"

"Cut the bull, Marisa."

"You can stand there and look me in the eye and tell me that I don't love you?"

"Maybe you do. I have no way of knowing whatever it is you feel or whatever you want to name it. Let's just say I don't want any part of this wondrous love you keep throwing around. It's too damned painful. You ripped my insides out, lady, when you threw the job in my face and walked away. I was brand-new in a position of authority and responsibility. You didn't give me a chance to explain before you started giving me hell for being a chauvinist. You blamed me for everything any man had ever done or said to you that caused you to feel oppressed, from your father on."

"I was out of line," she murmured.

"No kidding." He spun away from her and strode across the room. He reached the window, glanced out, then spun to pace back toward her. "You gave me all kinds of grounds to fire you that day, but I didn't. I sat there and listened. I took it. Why? You wanna know why? Because I thought, believe it or not, that I would then get the same opportunity I was giving you to tell you what I thought about the situation, what I felt about your remarks, and what I felt about you. But you didn't give me that chance. Oh, no! You sailed out of there like a queen who'd effectively berated her serf. So I decided to give you a chance to simmer down. I thought by the next day we would both be calm enough that I could explain why I wanted you to work in Washington, why I thought we should spend some off-duty time together."

"I felt like such a fool when I got home that night," she admitted. "I'd made a complete ass of myself."

"If you're looking for an argument on that one, you won't get one from me."

She turned away, slowly walked over to the chair she'd recently left and sat down, resting her face in her hands. "Oh, Max. I've made such a mess of things!"

He hadn't moved. "I'll second that."

She glanced up at him, stung by his coldness. "Well, you don't walk on water, either, you know."

"I've never pretended I did. But I've always done my best to be straight with people. You've had almost six years to get over whatever was bugging you. Six years to get in touch with me, either by phone, letter, or personal visit. Six years, Marisa."

"I know that! You have no idea how many nights I lay in bed writing imaginary letters, making imaginary phone calls, visualizing myself visiting you with Timmy, introducing you to him..."

"What does he look like?"

The sudden conversational change caught her off guard. "What?"

"The question wasn't that difficult."

"Oh! Well, he's got blond hair. It's getting darker as he gets older. And his eyes are a sherry color, like yours."

Max turned away, so that she was staring at his back.

"He's about average height for his age, a little thin, a wiry build, I guess you'd say. Very active. He's—"

"Why didn't you tell me about him?" he said in a low voice, his back still to her.

"I didn't know how! How do you tell something like that...'you probably don't remember me, but'...or, 'Surprise'...or, 'by the way, Max, how do you feel about children'...or—"

He turned and looked at her in disgust. "Never mind. I get the picture."

She began to sob. "Damn...I was...determined not to...cry. I haven't...cried since I...found out he was...mis...sing. I reminded my...self that I was...a...pro...fessional...and I was...going to...find him...no matter...what!"

"Even if it meant asking me to help you."

"Yes. I mean, no, I didn't think about you at first. It was only…it was when I saw Troy talking to Harry and I…heard what they were saying…and I knew that something was drastically wrong…and that Troy was mixed up in something much worse than I could have imagined and that Harry was a part of it…and you trusted Harry and—"

He walked over to her. "Okay, okay, settle down, all right? You're right. I trusted Harry as much as I trusted anybody. He would have been one of the last ones I suspected. You may have saved a lot of lives by warning me when you did."

"But you may lose yours because I did!"

"I've lived with that risk for years. It comes with the territory."

She glanced around the room in despair. "So what are we going to do?"

He glanced over at the massive bed. "Get some sleep."

"Are you serious?"

"I couldn't be more serious. We're going to have to be ready when Harry gets here in the morning. That means we're going to have to be rested and alert. One point in our favor—according to Chasen, Harry intends to make our demise look like an accident. That will give us a little more opportunity to mess up his plans."

"Do you think Timmy is here?"

"My honest guess? No, I don't. I think Chasen wanted you to believe he has Timmy, but it wouldn't surprise me to learn that once you were over here Timmy was returned to your sister."

"She would have let me know."

"How?"

"I never thought of that. I could call her and ask. Oh, if only I knew he was all right I could rest easier. I've been so scared to even let myself think about what could have happened to him."

"Well, since our kind host has not seen fit to place a telephone at our disposal, you can shelve that idea for now." He walked over to the bed and pulled the spread down. "Do you have a problem with sharing the bed?" he asked without looking at her.

"I, uh, no, of course not. I, uh—"

"I give you my word that I will not touch you."

"Oh."

He'd been removing his shirt as he spoke, but her last monosyllable caused him to pause and look over his shoulder. "I'll be damned if you don't sound disappointed!"

"It's not that. I just thought about those days on the yacht when everything was so different between us."

He kicked off his shoes and stepped out of his pants before replying. "The reason for the way I behaved on board ship," he said crawling into bed without looking at her, "is quite simple. I was suffering from amnesia. I heard the doctor refer to me as your husband so I thought we were married.''

She stared at him in astonishment. "You mean, all that time you thought that I was—"

"I thought we'd taken a vacation as a sort of second honeymoon. It seemed logical and it fitted all the circumstances. And if you'll remember correctly, you certainly didn't fight me off."

She slipped out of the summer dress she wore, kicked off her sandals and padded to the other side of the bed. Max already had reason to know that George's daughter had a very provocative sense of style with regard to her underwear. He closed his eyes when she crawled into bed beside him.

"Max?"

"What?"

"I've never had any desire to fight you off. Not ever."

Why had she decided to give him that choice piece of news at that particular time?

He turned his back to her and pounded his pillow.

"Max?"

"What?"

"We could both be killed tomorrow."

"I'd say the odds are definitely in favor of that, yes."

"Do we have to go to sleep angry with each other?"

"I don't care how you go to sleep. Just do it."

"Max?"

"What!"

"I never wanted to hurt you."

"Oh, wow, Marisa. That makes everything okay then, doesn't it?"

"I love you, Max."

He didn't say anything.

"I believe in love. With all my heart. I believe that love can create miracles. I've seen it happen. I've felt it happen."

"Good, then love us up a miracle tomorrow and maybe we'll live to tell this to our grandchildren."

They were both silent, thinking of the implications of that last remark.

"Max, just hold me for a little while, all right? If you have to, pretend you're married to me again. I just don't want to be alone."

He heard the plea in her voice and almost groaned out loud. The woman had the damnedest ability to twist him around her little finger. No one had ever had that ability before or since. He hated it. He really did.

Then he rolled over and gathered her into his arms. They lay there together for several hours, neither one speaking, wondering what tomorrow would bring.

Max felt her body snuggled close to his before he surfaced from sleep. She felt so good to him, and she fitted the curl of his body as though made for him.

His arm was wrapped around her, hugging her closely against him.

What a hell of a time to find out that he was a father. He hadn't been in this much danger in years. He'd grown rusty, that was obvious by the way they had been so easily picked up and brought to their present location. He was past his prime and he knew it.

Because he had always been on his own, he'd never worried much about an assignment. He knew that he could be killed at any time, but so what? Everybody had to die sometime. In the meantime, he was doing something he enjoyed.

For the first time in his life he felt a strong desire to live, at least until he could see his son. He had a son. Timmy. Was that for Timothy? He wondered why she had chosen that name. Not that he would have wanted her to use his name. Maximilian was a mouthful. He'd never used his full name. Few people knew what it was, or that it was a family name.

He tried to picture his son. Did Marisa carry pictures of him? Even if she did, she wouldn't have them now. All she'd managed to hang on to was her passport.

She stirred against him, causing an immediate reaction within him. Not that he intended to do anything about it, but at least he knew he wasn't dead yet. If he had his way, he'd get through the next few hours, then head back to the States.

He wanted to live. Perhaps his determination would even the odds they had to face in the next few hours.

"Max?" she murmured in a sleepy voice.

"Yes?" He unconsciously tightened his arm around her midriff.

"I'm glad I'm with you. I've missed you so much these past few years. Being with you on the yacht was the most wonderful time of my life. It really was like a honeymoon."

"I know. I've been lying here thinking about it. Is there a chance you could be pregnant? I didn't think to protect you either time."

"No. It's not the right time, Max."

There was a knock on the door. Max rolled out of bed in one smooth movement, grabbed his pants and slipped them on before he said, "Yes?"

"Mr. O'Donnell has asked that we bring you downstairs" was the response.

"Give us five minutes, all right?"

"We'll tell him."

He turned to Marisa. "Not much time. I'll let you have the bathroom first."

She slipped out of bed and hurried to the adjoining room. Within a couple of minutes she came out and began to dress while he went inside. He looked into the mirror and rubbed his jaw. He didn't have time to shave. He'd have to go as he was.

Marisa was dressed and waiting for him when he reentered the bedroom. A moment later they heard another tap on the door. She reached for his hand. "Here we go," she said, taking a deep breath and exhaling with a gusty sigh.

"We'll do just fine. We've always made a great team. There's no reason to think we won't make it today."

Ten

Max saw Harry O'Donnell as soon as they arrived at the top of the staircase. O'Donnell stood with his back to them, speaking in low tones to one of the men standing guard by the door. He turned as soon as he heard them on the stairs.

"Good morning, Max. I hope you slept well."

Max didn't respond. He continued down the stairs with Marisa beside him. He studied his adversary carefully for any signs of weakness, but Harry was good. He showed nothing.

When they reached the massive foyer, Harry nodded to Marisa. "We meet again. You shouldn't have run away from us in Barcelona, you know. We would have been most willing to answer your questions."

Marisa stared at him without speaking. Never had Max been more proud of her. Her training served her well. Not by the tiniest movement did she show any sign of nervousness or apprehension.

"Not very talkative, are you, but then perhaps I wakened you too early. Sorry about that." He waved them into the salon where they had seen Troy the night before. "We're having coffee in here this morning."

Max squeezed Marisa's hand in reassurance and she looked at him with a serene smile. They were in this together, all the way.

"You've probably wondered why I've gone to so much trouble to have you visit me here in my home," Harry said, sitting in the wing chair across from the sofa where Max and Marisa had chosen to sit. A young girl in a maid's uniform came in bearing a large silver service. Harry motioned for her to place it on the table between the sofa and chairs.

How civilized we're being, Max thought to himself as he watched Marisa pour coffee in three cups and hand each man one of them. *We're so very proper as this jerk gloats over us.*

Harry didn't seem to be enjoying himself as much as he might have hoped. Obviously their lack of response was irritating him somewhat. Good. An

WHERE THERE IS LOVE 141

emotional man was easier to deal with because he wasn't thinking as clearly.

"I have you to thank for my home and fine surroundings, Max."

"Do you?"

Harry nodded, pleased once again. "You see, it was when you were promoted over me that I decided I'd had enough of playing the dedicated public servant. Or in our case, private servant. I deserved that promotion. Not you. I'd been with the Agency longer and accomplished a hell of a lot more than you ever did."

"I had no control over their choice, Harry. No more than you did."

Harry looked over at Marisa and smiled. "I obviously wasn't the only disgruntled one. You left not long after his promotion. You can imagine my shock when I learned that Troy's sister-in-law was Marisa Stevens, *the* Marisa Stevens I'd known in the Agency. And when he mentioned that you had given birth to a son a little less than nine months after leaving, it was easy enough to guess what had happened. You tried to trap Max into marrying you, and it didn't work." Harry laughed. "Even I knew his views on the subject of marriage. He's never bothered keeping them a secret."

"What's the point of this conversation, Harry?"

Harry smiled. "I'm just enjoying the various nuances of this unique situation. You've been getting in my way these past couple of years, Max. I had to take out a few men with whom I'd worked amicably and it irritated me. I won't mind getting rid of you."

"Do you really think no one else knows about you, Harry?"

"Ah, but you don't have proof of anything. After your death, evidence linking you to certain... misadventures... will be discovered."

Max laughed.

The muscles in Harry's face tightened. "I'm so glad that I afford you so much entertainment." O'Donnell came to his feet. "Your deaths will be reported as an unfortunate accident. A couple of tourists traveling too fast on the winding coastline roads. It's easy to miscalculate a curve and go over the edge. It happens all too frequently."

"A fine plan, except for one minor problem."

"Which is?"

"Getting us into the car in the first place."

Harry's smile widened. "Oh, that won't be a problem at all. You see, you'll both be unconscious when you're placed in the car."

"I see."

"We've covered every possible eventuality. Why, I'll be one of the most visible mourners at the funerals. Two fellow agents on vacation. I might even mention that you had stopped by to spend the night with me while touring the countryside."

"And the car?"

"Already rented in your name."

"Ingenious."

"I agree."

Marisa leaned forward. "Where is Troy?"

"Earning his keep. Your visit has been a trifle awkward due to the timing. We expected you to show up several days ago."

"I take it you have a shipment coming in."

O'Donnell smiled once again. "I haven't the foggiest idea what you're talking about. I'm a U.S. agent, Max. You know that. Anything more would be a conflict of interest."

"Try treason."

O'Donnell chuckled. "Even more dramatic, but hardly accurate."

"We'll let a jury of your peers make that decision."

"Don't you wish, Max. Don't you wish."

The door opened behind them and Harry looked up. One of O'Donnell's men said, "We've brought both cars around."

"Good, good. We need to take care of this matter as soon as possible." He motioned for them to stand. "Sorry to rush you like this."

Max knew what they had to do, and he knew he could count on Marisa. Without looking at her he strode toward the door, knowing she was somewhere behind him. The man at the door turned just as Max's foot hit the door, slamming it, while his arm came around the man's throat. He hooked his foot around the man's ankle and pushed, placing him in a vise. With his other hand he reached inside the man's coat and removed the pistol hanging in his shoulder holster and then turned both the man and himself to face the room.

All of this happened within five seconds.

Marisa barreled into O'Donnell's chest, catching him off balance, and with a practiced grip on his arm and shoulder, threw him over her shoulder so that he landed on top of the table holding the silver service.

The clatter was immensely satisfying to Max, who watched with the pistol in his hand.

Marisa found O'Donnell's pistol and held it on him, standing with her legs spread, both arms gripping the handle of the pistol.

Max shoved the pistol he was holding into the side of the man he'd disarmed and said, "Get over against the wall."

Keeping his eye on the man, he walked over to the rope pull that signaled the help, and tugged it.

In less than a minute the maid opened the door and came in. Her eyes widened when she saw the two men being held at gunpoint. Max smiled at her. Her eyes got larger.

"I'm afraid we made a mess of that lovely service you brought in earlier. Would you mind asking the chef to prepare more coffee, and perhaps something to eat. We missed our evening meal and are a little hungry."

The young woman scurried out while Marisa began to laugh.

Harry seemed to have regained some of the breath that had been knocked out of him when Marisa had launched herself into his rib cage. He no longer lay gasping in the shattered remains of the coffee table, silver service and china. "You're insane, Max."

Max didn't bother to reply. He just waited.

Within minutes the door opened once again. This time the maid was accompanied by four men, one of whom was obviously the chef. The other three appeared to be kitchen and garden help.

The chef took in the scene before nodding to Max. "Doesn't look as though you've lost your touch, boss. I couldn't have done it better myself."

"I'm glad you approve," Max responded drily, as the kitchen help pulled out handcuffs for O'Donnell and his henchman. "It took you long enough to get here."

"Hey, you're the one who wanted to play it this way. We were ready to take him last night."

Harry stood, his hands locked in front of him, and glared around him. "Who the hell are these people?"

Max smiled. "Oh, just some of my former agents. My boss let me know yesterday that he'd called in some of my most effective, but unfortunately retired, men. None of them ever worked in your sector, so I knew you wouldn't recognize them."

He walked over to Harry. "Let me introduce you." He nodded toward the man by the door. "The tall, black-haired, bearded one is Quinn McNamara, lieutenant colonel, retired, of the United States Air Force." He nodded to the two men who had handcuffed the man at the door. "The red-haired gentleman with the unrepentent grin on his face is Tim Walker, who currently resides in Colorado, his sidekick is Steve Donovan who did some work for me at one time in addition to his duties as a television news reporter."

Glancing at the man who stood beside Marisa, he said, "This man is Joel Kramer, now best known for turning out thriller novels based on some of his less savory adventures."

He looked at Harry for a long moment before he continued. "I know my reputation in the department with regard to the subject of marriage. These men preferred home life to what you and I chose, Harry, but they were prevailed upon to help us set the trap." He turned back to Quinn. "What's going on outside?"

The dark-haired man replied, "All of his people have been rounded up. We're watching his business associate. We'll be in on the arrival of the shipment that's due tonight."

"Thanks, guys, for pitching in like this. I wasn't certain if you'd be available when I mentioned your names to the boss earlier."

"You think you're so damned smart!" Harry snarled, standing between Marisa and Joel. "You think you've managed to get off scot-free. Well, I'm not going alone, you son of a—" With a flick of his wrist Harry pulled out a small pistol no larger than his palm and fired at Max, who was standing less than three feet away.

Max saw the movement and heard the explosion at the same time he felt the bullet hit his chest. There was no pain at first. He felt as though a hand had punched him hard, taking his breath away. He saw Joel grab Harry and wrest the gun away from him, saw Marisa run to him calling his name, heard the commotion behind him.

All he could think about as he felt his knees crumple beneath him was *I never did get to meet my son.*

Eleven

———

"Daddy, why did you leave me?"

"Mommy, where are you?"

"Daddy, when are you coming back to go fishing? I've been waiting to go with you. I'll never go with anyone else, Daddy. Just you."

"Amanda? Come here, sweetie. Come to Maxie. See, Mom? She can walk. Watch her walk to me, Mom."

"Leave me alone. You're not my family. I don't have a family. Go play with your own kids."

"Don't touch me. Just leave me alone. No, I don't want to go play with the others."

"I'm not wearing those stupid clothes. I don't care where you got them. I can buy my own stuff. Just leave me alone."

"I don't care what you think. I didn't take your dumb earrings. Why would I want them? How come I'm the one you always ask when something is missing?"

"I don't care what time it is. I'll come home whenever I feel like it. You're not my boss."

"Get out of my room. You have no right to go through my things. No right! Can't a person have a little privacy?"

"Don't play tough with me, Julio. I'm not impressed. You're nothing but a two-bit punk. I've had tougher guys than you for breakfast. Now get lost!"

"Listen. This is my place, you hear me? It's not much but I pay the rent for this room, so you get the hell out and leave me alone."

"Aw, Johnny, I can't go back to school. It's been too long, man. I've been out too long. Give me a break, Johnny."

"Hey, Johnny, just wanted to let you know. I got accepted at UCLA. Yeah, no kidding. So, what do you think? Will I ever fit the part of big man on campus?"

* * *

"Max, can you hear me? Max, this is Marisa. Oh, Max, please hang in there. I know it's tough. I know you're really hurting, but I need you . . . and Timmy needs you, too. I want you to get better so I can yell at you again. I want you to yell at me. I deserve it. I got you into this mess. Oh, Max, please don't give up!"

"Max? This is Joel. I really feel rotten about this. Guess I've been out of the business for too long. I never thought to look for a hidden weapon. Man, he was quick.

"Look, all the guys are here to see how you're doing. I'm going to go now so that they can see you. Hang in there, buddy. You can make it. You're the toughest one of the bunch!"

"As you can see, there was considerable damage done to the chest area. The bullet barely missed the heart. The lung was punctured but seems to be responding nicely now.

"He came through surgery, which was a miracle in itself. He'd lost a considerable amount of blood. As soon as he was stabilized they flew him from France to our private hospital.

"He'd recently received a severe blow to the head that had weakened him considerably. We think it's a miracle that he's still alive."

* * *

"Where there is love, Max, miracles can happen.

"It was a miracle that he survived surgery.

"It was a miracle he's still alive.

"Love can work miracles, Max. You just have to believe in them."

"Hang in there, buddy. You can make it. I know you can."

"Timmy's waiting to meet you, Max. He really needs you in his life. So do I, love. So do I."

"Run along and play, Maxie. Mommy's got to get the baby down for her nap."

"Yes, you may feed your sister, but try not to make a mess."

"Here, Max. Hold still. We want to get a picture of the two of you together. Now, then. That's it."

"No school for the next three months? Won't that be fun? A chance to play every day. And when you go back to school in September, you'll be a big old second grader. It won't be long until you've grown up big and tall, as big as your daddy."

"Mommy loves you, darling."

"Hey, big man, your dad loves you."

"See, Amanda loves you, too."

"I love you, Max."

"I love you."

"Love creates miracles. You can make it."

* * *

The first time he opened his eyes, the bright lights blinded him. He closed his eyes and kept them closed for a long time. Or at least what seemed like a long time.

The second time he opened his eyes, the room was in shadow. He kept his eyes open and looked around the hospital room. He was alone. There was a rustling sound like water trickling, as well as a steady beep from somewhere close by.

He was alive and hooked up to all sorts of machines. He started to wonder what time it was, but fell asleep before the thought was completed.

The next time he opened his eyes, he saw Marisa, sitting beside the bed and holding his hand. He attempted to tighten his grip and discovered how weak he was. Even that small movement caught her attention and she glanced at his face.

"Hi," she said in a whisper. She tried to smile but her mouth quivered.

She looked like hell. She was pale, and there were dark smudges beneath her eyes. She had lost weight, so that her cheekbones were more prominent than before, which drew attention to her eyes.

He licked his lips in an effort to moisten them. "This is getting to be a habit, me laid up in some bed." His voice sounded rusty from disuse.

"How are you feeling?"

He tried to smile, but wasn't certain of his success. "Like I was shot."

"I'm so sorry," she whispered.

"It wasn't your fault."

"Oh, but it was. I was the one who got you involved in this mess."

"No. It was all part of my job. What happened after I went down?"

"I thought those friends of yours were going to rip Harry apart. The shots caused the men on the outside to come running. We must have had twenty people on that case."

He closed his eyes, thinking about his superior's decision to call in all the troops. So he hadn't completely relied on Max's reassurances that he could handle the situation. There were times when it felt good to be outguessed.

"Why don't you sleep now?" she whispered when he started to speak.

"I need to know what happened."

She stroked his hand. "Some of the men took charge of Harry while the rest were determined to get you to medical attention." She looked away, then back at him. "Even though Harry was thoroughly searched, he obviously had hidden a capsule of cyanide. They found him dead in his cell the next morning."

So it was over. Harry was gone, the smuggling ring that they had been after for so long appeared to be stopped.

"What about Troy?"

"Unfortunately, he got caught in the crossfire between our people and the men bringing the cargo in. He was killed instantly."

"How is your sister taking it?"

"It was a shock to her, of course, but she said that she felt a certain amount of relief. She had discovered some time ago that he wasn't the man she had thought he was when they married. They had not been getting along. She was afraid of him. He'd made it clear that he wouldn't consider a divorce."

"No wonder. He didn't want his financial situation to be scrutinized."

The soft whoosh of the door opening caused them to look up. A bright-eyed nurse came in. "Mr. Moran, you need to rest. The monitors are showing an increased pulse rate." She smiled at Marisa. "I'm sure you understand."

"Are you coming back?" he asked, trying to sound nonchalant.

"Yes" was all she said.

He smiled and was immediately asleep.

Marisa left the hospital, feeling a sense of hopefulness that she had not had since Max had been shot. She would never forget the horror of that moment, or the days and nights of wondering if he was going to make it.

She had no more reason to stay. In fact, she needed to return to Seattle and Timmy, although Eileen insisted that he was doing fine with her and that there was no reason to be concerned.

Max had been right. Timmy had been returned to Eileen the day after Marisa had left. He'd been full of excited tales about all the things he'd done with one of the men who worked in Troy's warehouse. He'd never understood what had happened.

Now, at last, Max knew of Timmy's existence. She wished he had learned about his son in another way, but there was no point worrying about that now.

When Max was recovered, they would talk about his meeting Timmy. Timmy was such an outgoing little guy that he'd probably take to Max with no problem.

The problem was how Max was going to respond to the little boy. She knew that Max had been alone most of his life. He'd never allowed anyone to get close to him. Would having a son make a difference to him?

Only time would tell.

He felt as weak as a three-day-old baby and he hated it. Everything irritated him—most especially, the insistent cheerfulness of the nurses. When the door opened again, he scowled.

"What a picture of cheerful recuperation you make," Marisa said, coming in the door.

"I'm fed up with cheerfulness!"

"I see they have you up now." He was sitting in a large overstuffed chair by the window.

"Not fast enough to suit me."

"My, we are in rare form today."

"Now don't you start on me. I've had it up to here with bossy females telling me what to do."

She smiled and sat down in the straight-back chair by the bed. "I know. You're used to being the one giving the orders. Not much fun when you're on the receiving end."

He crossed his arms and glared at her. When she continued to smile, he relented. "What's that you're wearing?"

She glanced down at the dress she'd bought the day before. She'd been forced to buy a small wardrobe since her belongings had been shipped from Barcelona to Seattle. She started to explain, when he said, "Not the dress. I'm talking about the perfume."

"Just something I picked up, why?"

"No reason. You're looking more rested these days. How are you feeling?"

"Much better, now that you're improving."

They stared at each other for a moment before Max dropped his gaze. "There's no reason for you to be hanging around here. Shouldn't you be with Timmy?"

"Yes. That's one of the things I came to tell you. I need to get back to Seattle. School is starting soon. I need to plan my classes."

"So you came to say goodbye."

"That's right. And to invite you to come visit us when you're feeling better."

"I don't think that's such a good idea."

"Why not?"

"You've got your own life. You and Timmy have done just fine without me. There's no reason for me to confuse him."

"Max?"

"What?"

"I've told Timmy that you're his father, that you were hurt and that I was staying here until I was certain you were out of danger."

"You did what? Why would you do such a thing? Especially now. You never bothered to tell him about me before, so why—"

"I didn't tell him before because I was a coward. I ran from a situation I didn't know how to handle. I hope I've matured a little since then. Besides, things are different now."

"What do you mean?"

She grinned. "I know how you feel about me."

"So?" he asked belligerently.

"Max," she said in a patient voice, "I love you very much. I understand that you don't have any reason to trust or believe in love, but I have enough trust for both of us. The most important thing is that you're alive. The rest can be worked out."

She stood and walked over to him. "They say that grouchiness is a sign of recovery. If that's the case you're doing great!" She leaned down and kissed him very lightly on the lips. "Take care of yourself. Call me when you can. I hope you'll consider coming to Seattle for a visit soon."

He watched her walk out of the room, out of his life, and he wanted to yell at her to leave him alone. He didn't need her in his life. He didn't need anyone in his life. He was used to being alone. He much preferred it.

The ache in his chest was due to his recent injury. He'd get over it and resume his life. Nothing had changed. Nothing at all.

Twelve

———

"**Y**ou wanted to see me?" Max asked, standing in front of his superior's desk.

"Sit down, Max" was the reply.

He would rather face a firing squad than the upcoming interview.

"How are you feeling?"

"I'm making it."

"You came back to work too soon."

"I'm all right."

"Didn't the doctors suggest you give yourself a couple of months to fully recover?"

"I was going crazy, sitting around my place doing nothing."

"Then I would suggest that this is a good time for you to take a vacation."

"I never take vacations, you know that."

"Perhaps it's time for you to consider developing new habits."

"I can't just walk away from my job, sir."

"Are you under the impression that you're indispensable?"

"Obviously not. You've gotten along without me for several weeks now."

"Galling, isn't it?"

"I don't know what you mean."

"You've made this job your life, Max. How long have you been with the Agency?"

"Almost twenty years."

"You could consider retirement, you know."

"And do what?"

"Develop some hobbies, perhaps? Get married? Have a family?"

"What has Marisa said to you?" he asked suspiciously.

Obi-wan gave him a beatific smile. "Ah, so you have someone already in mind."

"Absolutely not. No, sir, I don't. I mean, I'm willing to face up to my responsibilities. I've already set up a monthly income for her and the boy, and—"

"Are you saying you have a son, Max?"

"Didn't you know?"

"Despite my reputation, I am not omniscient" was the reply. "How old is your son?"

"Five."

"A delightful age. I take it that he's Marisa's child?"

"Yes."

"Well, then, it looks as though you've managed to get a head start on that family!"

"You don't understand . . . sir. I mean, I know nothing about this fathering business. I lost my parents when I was quite young. I haven't been in a family environment for years. I'm not husband material, that's all. As for being a father—"

"Obviously, you've given the matter considerable thought."

"I've thought of nothing else since I found out about the boy. If I thought I could be the father he needs, of course I'd do whatever was necessary. But I can't just—"

"Have you met the boy?"

"No, sir."

"Well, then. Your course is clear. Take some time off, go to Marisa—she's in Seattle, didn't you say?—and get acquainted with your offspring."

"But, sir—"

"That's a direct order, Max." The man behind the desk looked at his calendar. "Report to me again on November first."

"*November!* That's almost three months . . . sir."

"Goodbye, Max. Have a safe journey. Be sure to give Marisa my regards."

Who did he think he was, *God?* muttered Max to himself as he returned to his office. Nobody could force him to do anything. He could resign. That's what he'd do. Resign.

Yeah, he missed her. He couldn't deny that. Despite everything he could do, his thoughts continued to return to those days they had spent on the yacht, when he had felt young and free to love Marisa in every way possible.

He'd wake up in the middle of the night, dreaming of making love to her. Her response to his lovemaking haunted him.

He'd thought about asking her to move back to D.C. but had eventually discarded the idea. She had a full and satisfying life in Seattle. Besides, she'd never hinted that she would consider the possibility of such a move.

Max reached his office and opened the door. Two workmen were in there.

"What's going on?"

One of them looked around. "We're moving everything out of this room. We have orders to paint and recarpet."

His boss never left anything to chance. Max took a few of his personal belongings out of the desk and left the building.

* * *

When he landed at the Seattle-Tacoma airport, it was raining. He had decided against calling Marisa to tell her he was coming. He wasn't absolutely certain he was going to see her. He might charter a boat, sail through the San Juan Islands, do a little fishing.

He hated to fish.

So maybe he'd drop by her place for a limited visit. He knew the address by heart. It would be the polite thing to do, as long as he was this close.

He retrieved his luggage from the carousel and walked outside. When a taxi pulled up, he got in and gave the driver Marisa's address.

Might as well get the visit behind him.

She probably wasn't home. It was Saturday. She was probably running errands or shopping. He'd leave a note to let her know he was in town.

By the time the taxi reached the Seattle suburb where Marisa lived, the rain had stopped, and in the thin, watery sunshine drops of water gleamed on every surface.

Max paid the driver, grabbed his bag and got out.

The house was Victorian, with gingerbread trim. He glanced around, studying the street that seemed filled with trees. In some ways it reminded him of the house in Southern California where he'd lived with his parents—large lawns fenced in, roses climbing fenceposts and porches.

A quiet place. A safe place for children.

He made himself pick up his bag and walk up to her porch. Without hesitating, he rang the doorbell. The front door was filled with a frosted-glass pane. He could see nothing inside.

He reached for the buzzer again. Before his finger came into contact with the surface, the door slowly swung open.

Max started to speak, then realized there was no one there.

"Hello," came a small voice.

Max glanced downward and saw a small boy peering up at him under a mop of wavy, light brown hair. The eyes were the same color as those he stared into each morning in the mirror.

He froze. He could feel his pulse rate jump and perspiration break out on his forehead.

"Hi," he managed to reply.

"What do you want?"

"I, uh— Is your mother at home?"

"Yes."

They both waited.

"May I speak to her?" Max finally asked.

"Just a minute," the little boy said, then closed the door in Max's face.

Max stood there, undecided. Should he wait or ring the doorbell again? Obviously Marisa had trained her son not to allow strangers into the house, which was good.

There was no doubt that he was a stranger.

He had turned away to look out at the street once more when he heard the door swing open. "I'm sorry about leaving you out on the—" she began to say. Then she saw who it was. "Max! Omigod! I can't believe it! You're here!" She launched herself into his arms.

He drew her tightly against him and kissed her the way he'd been dreaming about for weeks. She felt wonderful in his arms—warm and vital, and he could smell that wonderful scent she'd been wearing at the hospital.

When she finally pulled far enough away to take a deep breath, she hugged him fiercely to her. "Why didn't you tell me you were coming? Oh, this is wonderful! Come in, come in. I didn't mean for you to stand out here on the porch."

She took his hand and led him into the entryway. He glanced around, seeing highly polished wood and gleaming brass, hardwood floors with bright scatter rugs and a stairway that led to the floor above.

"When did you get here? How long can you stay? Oh, where did Timmy go? I want you to meet him."

Max grinned. He was feeling better by the minute. "I just got off the plane and I've made no plans at all. I've been kicked out of my office and ordered not to return to work until the first of November."

"Oh, that's wonderful!"

"It's going to take a little getting used to."

She led him into a large room that seemed to have a multitude of windows covered with some kind of gauzy material that allowed the light to come through. "Have you eaten? Would you like some coffee?"

"Coffee sounds good."

"Then let's go into the kitchen. Timmy? Come here, sweetheart. There's somebody I want you to meet."

Why had he thought this was going to be so difficult? Max asked himself several hours later. They'd just finished a wonderful meal. He couldn't remember the last time he'd had a home-cooked meal.

He was having difficulty visualizing this same woman tossing a man almost twice her size over her shoulder. Watching her with Timmy caused him to ache with an incomprehensible emotion.

He found Timmy fascinating.

"More pie, Max?" she was asking, bringing him out of his reverie.

"Oh, no, thank you."

He watched Timmy industriously clean his plate and smiled at the recent memory of being introduced to his son.

Timmy had come back from where he'd been playing when she called him. Marisa had knelt beside him and said, "Do you remember when I called you and said I was visiting with your daddy in Washington, D.C.?''

He eyed Max speculatively, then nodded. This kid was no dummy. He knew something was up.

"Well, he's come to visit us."

Max didn't know what to do. He knew nothing about kids. He could scarcely recall his own childhood.

They looked at each other in complete silence.

Marisa chuckled. "Come on, guys. I've got homemade cookies." She ruffled Timmy's mop of hair. "How about a glass of milk?"

He nodded, but he didn't take his eyes off Max.

They'd spent most of the day that way, allowing Marisa to fill in the silences with light conversation. She acted as though a man met his son every day. As though it was no big deal.

Now that they were finishing dinner, Max realized that he'd begun to relax. There was something about the homey atmosphere and Marisa's nonchalance that soothed him.

"Why don't you guys go into the living room while I clear the table."

"Let me help," Max offered, preferring to do anything rather than make conversation with the little boy whose gaze never seemed to leave him.

"Oh, that's all right. It won't take a minute. Go ahead." She made a shooing gesture toward the living room where Timmy had already gone.

Max reluctantly followed.

He sat on the sofa and watched Timmy hook up a miniature train that had been hand carved.

"Where did you get your train?"

"My aunt Eileen gave it to me for my birthday."

"When is your birthday?"

"June twenty-seventh."

"You're five now?"

"Uh-huh."

End of conversation.

Max was way over his head and he knew it. He just didn't know where to go from here.

"My mom says you work to get rid of bad guys and that you're really brave."

"Does she?"

"Uh-huh. And she said a bad guy shooted you in the chest and that you was sick for a long time."

"That's true."

"Does it still hurt?"

"Not much."

"That's good." He began to pull his train along the blue-striped border of the large area rug. He made the first circuit in silence before he spoke again. "Are you really my daddy?"

Here it comes. "Yes, I am."

"How come I never saw you before?"

Good question. "Well, I guess it's because I work long hours and never took the time to come out to see you."

"Oh. Didn't you want to see me?"

Now how did he handle that one? "Yes. I wanted to see you very much." He recognized the truth in his words as he spoke them. From the moment he'd learned about Timmy he'd felt a yearning to see him. But he'd been afraid. He was still afraid, but he wasn't certain what was causing his fear.

"I wanted to see you, too," Timmy said with a nod and began the second circuit of his train around the room.

"You did?"

"Uh-huh. I didn't know where you lived or anything. I thought you might live somewhere close. But Mom said you lived a long way away and that someday we could go visit you, but she never said when."

"Timmy?" Marisa called from the other room. "Come on. It's time to get ready for bed, darling."

His son got a pained expression on his face so familiar to Max that he almost laughed out loud. He'd caught a glimpse of the same expression on his own face more than once.

There was no way that Marisa could have forgotten the father of her child. Not with so many reminders.

"I have to go to bed now," Timmy said with commendable resignation. "Will you be here tomorrow?"

"I might be," Max offered cautiously.

"Good," Timmy replied with satisfaction. "I'd like that."

"You would?"

"Uh-huh. If it isn't raining tomorrow, I can take you out to my backyard. I have this big tree house that my mom made for me. We sit up there sometimes and look out. Maybe you'd like to do that with me."

Max could scarcely swallow around the lump in his throat. He couldn't say anything, so he nodded.

"Timmy! Your bathwater's getting cold."

"See ya," Timmy said with a tiny smile on his face.

Once again Max couldn't say a thing.

"He told me you built him a tree house." He and Marisa were in the living room once again, while Timmy was sound asleep upstairs.

"Yes. I decided that every little boy deserved a tree house, even though Eileen is constantly worrying that he's going to fall out of it and break something."

"Weren't you afraid?"

"Terrified. But I also knew that I couldn't coddle him. He needed the space to grow without being smothered."

"You've done a wonderful job with him, Marisa."

"You have no idea how good it makes me feel to hear you say that. There were times when I was so scared and so uncertain of myself. I wanted to call you, to talk to you about him, to ask questions. There's so much I don't know."

"I don't, either. It's frightening to think about how much I don't know about children."

"The nice thing is that they're patient. They'll wait for you to learn." They were quiet for several moments before Marisa said, "I want to thank you for opening the account for Timmy. You didn't have to do that, you know."

"I would have done it sooner, if you'd told me about him."

"You're never going to forgive me for that, are you?"

"It's not that, exactly. I just feel that I'm starting out as a parent five years behind."

"You'll do fine, Max. I know you will. We can work out a schedule where he can come to visit you whenever you have the time for him. Just think of all the things you can show him, particularly when he gets older. He'll have the best of both of our worlds. It will work out, I know it will."

She was saying all the right things, answering questions that he'd thought about but hadn't known how to bring up. Now that she was making it easy for him, he could relax, knowing that things were working out.

Couldn't he?

"I don't think that's going to work, Marisa. I've been on my own too long. I wouldn't know how to look after a child."

Thirteen

Marisa heard his words with a sinking heart. He'd been unusually quiet all day, but she had put that down to his normal reticence and the strangeness of being in her home and seeing Timmy for the first time.

"I see" was all she could say.

"I want to do more with Timmy. It's just that I don't know how. I haven't a clue how to behave around him."

"You did just fine today."

"Because you were here."

"Well, once you get used to him, maybe—"

"The thing is, I don't want to ship him back and forth between us. I think he deserves two parents who live together and look after him together."

Marisa stiffened, wondering if she was understanding him correctly. This was Max, the man who blew up whenever any of his men decided to marry. Surely he couldn't be suggesting that—

"I think we should get married."

He was. He was actually suggesting marriage.

"Oh, Max." He looked so tortured, like a man facing the agonies of a dental chair. She wrapped her arms around his neck and kissed him. Never had she seen him any more tense than he was at the moment.

She teased him by running her tongue across his bottom lip. He groaned and gathered her close to him. "Oh, God, honey. I've missed you so damned much." He buried his face against her neck.

"Max. Marrying me would go against all of your principles."

"I don't care," he muttered in a muffled voice.

"We live on opposite coasts."

"Mm-hm." He began to nibble on her ear.

"We can't just— Mm, Max, that feels so good."

He finally drew away and looked at her. "I know there are things to work out between us. But we owe it to Timmy to try. We brought him into this world. He deserves the best the two of us can give him."

"Is that the reason you want to marry me?"

"I'm not going to lie to you. The thought of marriage sends cold chills down my spine. I've got almost two months before I go back to work. I thought we could use the time to get better acquainted. I'd like Timmy to get used to me and I need time to get used to him. Meanwhile—" He began to kiss her along her jawline.

"Meanwhile?" she managed to ask.

"Maybe you can help me learn to be around little boys."

"You'll do fine."

When his mouth found hers, she melted against him, eager for his touch. When he finally pulled away from her, she lay against his shoulder, her eyes closed.

"I need to leave."

"You can always stay here," she said with a dreamy smile.

"I don't think that's a good idea."

She opened her eyes slowly. "Why not?"

"I think it would be confusing for Timmy. He needs to adjust to the idea of having me around more often on a gradual basis."

She sighed. "I suppose you're right." She studied him for a moment. "Max?"

He lifted his brows in inquiry.

"Are you sure that you want this?"

"Honey, I'm not sure about anything at this point. My entire life has been turned upside down. All I know is my job and it's just been moved out of my reach for three months. I'm drifting out to sea without a rudder or a paddle. All I could think about on the flight out here was that for the first time in my life, I have a place to go and people to see. I find that really scary.''

"But you're not afraid of anybody, Max. You faced dangerous men on a regular basis for years. What's so frightening now?''

"I'm out of my element. I have nothing to offer you or Timmy. It surprises me that you haven't found someone else in all this time.''

"I never wanted anyone else, even when I knew I didn't have a chance with you.''

He kissed her again, slowly and with great thoroughness. "I need to go.''

"If you insist on leaving, I want you to take my car.''

"But won't you need it?''

"Not before morning. Then we'll have to decide a few things. If you're on vacation, then I want you to enjoy yourself.''

He smiled, a slow, masculine smile that made her heart race.

"What I mean is,'' she hastened to add, "you've told me that you've never taken a vacation before. So we need to plan some trips. Maybe travel over to Vancouver Island on the weekends when I can go with you. Perhaps during the weekdays you and

Timmy can spend some time together, get acquainted."

He nodded slowly. "I suppose."

She grinned. "You might try a little more enthusiasm."

Max shook his head. "I'm really way over my head on this one."

She gave him a quick kiss. "I have faith in you. Tomorrow we'll find you a place to stay not far from here, maybe get a rental car. What do you think?"

"I think I'm glad I came here."

She hugged him. "So am I. I'm going to show you that being a daddy and eventually a husband can be fun."

"Did you like to play ball when you was a kid?" Timmy asked around a mouthful of hamburger.

Max studied the earnest face across the table in the fast-food restaurant where he and Timmy were indulging themselves after spending a couple of hours at the zoo.

"Uh, yes. I guess maybe I did."

"Can't you 'member?" Timmy asked sympathetically.

"Well, that was a long time ago, I have to admit."

With a wise nod, Timmy suggested, "Back when there was dinosaurs and monsters and things, right?"

Max choked on his drink. "Not quite *that* long ago." He wiped some ketchup from Timmy's chin and silently handed him his drink.

During the two weeks he'd been in Seattle, Max had spent part of each day with Timmy. Marisa had been right. He was beginning to understand the boy and that scared the hell out of him. Feeling vulnerable was not a condition he enjoyed. Having a five-year-old walking around with Max's heart firmly clasped in his small hand made him more than a little nervous.

He also realized that he had been getting in touch with his own childhood once again. This time he was remembering fewer of the painful memories and more of the pleasurable ones.

One day he'd bought a kite and Timmy had helped him to put the wretched thing together. He'd been reminded of the many times his dad had patiently worked with him on similar projects. Suddenly his parents seemed to be very close and very real to him. Long-forgotten conversations were surfacing, and he was getting in touch with the young boy inside of him that had hidden away in fear and panic. Timmy was coaxing him out to play.

Max didn't know what he would have done without Marisa. She continued to be nonchalant about the whole process of getting to know Timmy, ignoring Max's awkwardness.

Max felt as though he'd been an emotional cripple for years, as though he'd packed his emotions away and was only now rediscovering them. He was scared, but for the first time in a long while Max felt truly alive.

Now he stared across the table, able to recognize by his expression that Timmy was about to ask another of his innumerable questions.

"Was you ever a soldier?"

"Of sorts, I suppose. I wore a uniform for a couple of years."

Timmy appeared to accept his response, for which Max was grateful. He never knew what to expect from the boy.

"I'm going to be a soldier when I get big," Timmy announced with an emphatic nod, "and kill lots of bad guys."

"Bloodthirsty little guy, aren't you?" Max muttered.

"Huh?"

"Nothing. Are you about through with your hamburger?" Max looked at the meat and bread, all that Timmy had wanted at a place that bragged about putting everything on a burger. Preoccupied by his unrelenting and eternal quest for knowledge, Timmy had managed to take only two bites.

Timmy studied his burger for a moment, then resolutely picked it up and took a giant bite. Max had visions of the child choking and frantically tried to recall the Heimlich maneuver in case he was called upon to save his son's life.

His son. He found himself staring at the mop of unruly hair, the big eyes, the turned-up nose with its faint scattering of freckles and felt a warmth in his chest that spread throughout him. He smiled.

"Have you ever killed anyone?" Timmy asked after he swallowed.

Fortunately, Max had already finished his meal by that time or he might have needed some medical assistance himself. He forced himself not to show more than polite interest in the question.

"No one who readily comes to mind."

"Oh."

Damned if he didn't sound disappointed!

"My friend Davey said that his dad was in the army and fought in Nam." Timmy frowned. "Do you know Nam?"

"I've heard it mentioned once or twice," Max replied drily.

"Davey says his dad kilt lots of people. Sometimes his dad still dreams about it."

"Yeah, that can happen."

"I don't think I'd like that."

"No."

In a sudden shift of mood, Timmy brightened. "Do you like to fish?"

Max eyed him warily. "Why do you ask?"

"Davey and his dad go fishing all the time."

Max saw the trap that yawned widely before him. He just didn't know what to do about it. "Do they?" he asked in as noncommittal a tone as possible.

"Uh-huh. Once they took me with them out on this big boat."

"Did you enjoy it?"

Timmy's eyes sparkled. "Oh, yes."

"Did you fish?"

"Nah. I just watched."

"Do you like to fish?"

Timmy shrugged in elaborate unconcern. "I dunno. Nobody ever teached me how."

Max knew he could let it go. He could distract Timmy in several ways, but he knew what his son was trying to tell him. Over the past weeks he had learned to recognize the nuances of Timmy's seemingly unrelated questions. Timmy wanted a father. He wanted someone about whom he could talk with his friends.

For years Timmy had listened and learned about fathers and what they did and who they were. He'd listened but he'd had nothing to share. Until now.

"Would you like me to teach you how to fish?"

Timmy's eyes grew big. "You know how?"

"My dad taught me when I was about your age."

"And you'd teach me?" he asked in wonderment.

Max could feel his heart racing, his pulse pounding, and he knew his forehead was damp. "I'll teach you."

Once again Max approached Marisa's front door. More than two months had passed since the first time, but he was just as nervous.

He rang the bell. When the door swung open he immediately looked down at the small boy standing there.

"Daddy!"

Max felt his breath catch in his throat. The eagerness with which Timmy greeted him continued to astound him. He wasn't sure whether he would ever be able to take for granted hearing his son call him by that name.

"Hello, Timmy. You're looking remarkably well groomed."

Timmy eyed him suspiciously, then glanced down at his new shoes, pants, shirt and jacket before he asked, "What does that mean?"

Max grinned and picked him up, hugging him. "It means that I didn't expect you to stay so clean."

Timmy draped his arm around Max's neck and nodded. "Yeah. Mom said I was going to be in big trouble if I got dirty."

"And what would that be?"

Timmy cocked his head, thinking. "I pro'bly couldn't play in my tree house and stuff like that."

"That's quite a threat. I'll have to remember it for future use." He walked into the living room and sat down in one of the overstuffed chairs. Timmy leaned contentedly against him.

"You're going to sleep with my mommy," Timmy announced.

Max wondered if he would ever get used to Timmy's candid comments. "Is that so?"

Timmy nodded. "Yes. My mom said so."

"Well, then it must be true."

Timmy smiled. "I'm glad. Mommies and daddies are s'posed to sleep together."

"Ah."

"But first you're going to take a trip."

"That's true."

"Over to Victoria."

"Uh-huh."

"Without me."

The conversation was suddenly making sense. "Well, yes, we are, but we won't be gone long. We'll scout around to see all the fun things we can do so that the next time we go you'll go with us and we can do all those fun things together."

"Really?"

"Really."

"You promise not to have any fun without me?"

"I wouldn't think of it."

Max glanced up at the sound of Marisa's laughter as she walked into the room. She, too, was dressed in festive attire. She wore a white lace dress over a soft pink material that somehow made her skin glow. He wasn't sure how she did that. All he knew was that he loved her so much that his chest ached with the feeling.

"I'm not certain I like the idea of your promising not to have fun while you're with me."

Max grinned. "Well, there's fun and then there's fun."

Timmy climbed down from Max's lap. "Wow, Mom! You look like the Christmas angel on our tree!"

"I couldn't have said it better myself, Timmy," Max said, standing. "I take it you're ready."

She nodded. "I know this is going to sound ridiculous, but I'm really nervous."

"Join the club."

"I mean, I'm not nervous about what we're doing, it's just knowing that all those people are there, watching."

"You're the one who insisted on letting everybody know."

She nodded. "I told you I'm being silly and I know it."

Timmy took her hand. "If you don't want to go away, you can come to the movies with Auntie Eileen and me," he offered in a soothing manner.

Max saw the mischief gleam in Marisa's eyes as they met his. Damn, but he loved her sense of humor. She was waiting for him to comment, but he refused.

"Thank you for the invitation, Timmy. I'll get over being nervous, I'm sure."

Max wished he could be so sure about himself, but he didn't say anything. He knew that he wasn't going to change his mind. He just wanted the whole thing behind him.

He leaned over and kissed Marisa softly on the lips. Timmy giggled.

"Isn't there some rule that the groom isn't suppose to kiss the bride before the wedding?" she murmured when he lifted his head.

"I believe the tradition is that the groom is not to *see* the bride," he replied. "The way I look at it, we shot tradition all to pieces when we planned to take our five-year-old son to the wedding. But I absolutely draw the line about company on the honeymoon." He took Timmy's hand, then reached for Marisa with the other one. "C'mon. We've got people waiting to see if I'm actually going to go through with this. I wouldn't want to disappoint anybody!"

As soon as they pulled up in front of the small church, Max knew that their invitations hadn't been ignored by anyone. Not only were Marisa's sisters, Eileen and Julie, there, but he also spotted Quinn and Jennifer McNamara, Steve and Jessica Donovan, Tim and Elisabeth Walker, and Joel and Melissa Kramer. None of those men were ever going to let him forget what a rough time he'd given them for getting married and leaving the Agency. Was it any wonder that each of them had come to witness him metaphorically eat his words?

During the ensuing greetings and congratulations, and especially during Timmy's introduction to everyone, Max knew that he wouldn't have wanted it any other way. Somehow it seemed fitting to have them witness his change of heart.

He remembered the scenes when these former agents had come to tell him they were leaving the Agency and why. He remembered his cynicism and scorn at their utter conviction that what they were doing was right for them. Only now could he remember the patience and compassion he'd seen in their eyes at the time. He'd been puzzled then. Now he understood. Somehow he would have to find a way to apologize for his narrow vision. At long last, he was part of the group of men who were ready to admit to their vulnerability without fear of jeopardizing their strength.

The ceremony wasn't as painful as he had expected—nor was the informal reception and unmerciful teasing he received shortly thereafter. But he was more than ready to catch the small plane that flew them to Victoria at midafternoon.

When he closed the door to the honeymoon suite behind the courteous bellhop, Max felt as though the world had been locked out. For the first time in months, he and Marisa were finally alone.

She stood in the middle of the ornately decorated suite, glancing around. "The Canadians really know how to make you feel welcome, don't they?" she murmured, pointing to the bowl of fruit and a large arrangement of flowers.

Without commenting, Max walked over and slipped his arms around her waist. "Still nervous?" he asked in a low voice.

She gave a shaky laugh. "I'm not sure. I feel a little strange. I've never been married before."

"I have." She gave him a startled glance before he went on. "When I woke up on the yacht and heard you refer to me as your husband, I felt very married. As I recall, I complimented myself on my excellent taste." He brushed his lips across her cheeks. "I still do."

He could feel the tenseness in her body slowly leaving her. She wound her arms around his neck and hugged him. "Oh, Max! Thank you for saying that. I've been having the most horrific thoughts about having trapped you in some way. I didn't sleep at all last night thinking about it."

"I didn't sleep last night, either, but it wasn't because I was feeling trapped into anything."

She glanced up at him. "No?"

He pulled her closer so that her body was molded against him. "Uh-uh. I kept thinking of what I intended to do as soon as I finally got you alone."

She smiled up at him, her eyes shining.

"Come to think of it, how do couples ever get any privacy after their first child? It's a wonder there aren't more only children in this world!"

"Max?"

Why was she looking at him in such an amused way. "Yes?"

"You're already missing Timmy, aren't you?"

"Missing Timmy! Are you kidding? That kid can come up with questions faster than a Senate investigating committee, and every bit as penetrating. I feel as though I've been given a reprieve." He took her hand and drew her into the bedroom. "Of course I did think about how much he would have enjoyed the plane ride and the chance to see Puget Sound from the air. We'll have to go shopping tomorrow and maybe find him a souvenir for—" Marisa placed her fingers across his lips.

"I miss him, too, you know. But we'll be home in a couple of days."

He took his time removing her dress and underdress, treating her as though she were a gift-wrapped package that he was savoring. When he lifted her to place her on the bed, he had only to remove her shoes and panty hose. "Do you have any idea how much I love you?'' he whispered, stripping off his clothes and stretching out beside her.

''Care to show me?'' she whispered, while her hands lovingly explored him.

''I intend to spend the rest of my life showing you, starting now.''

* * * * *

SILHOUETTE® *Desire*™

CELEBRATES TEN YEARS OF HAPPY MARRIAGES WITH... JUNE GROOMS

COMING NEXT MONTH

#715 THE CASE OF THE CONFIRMED BACHELOR—
Diana Palmer MOST WANTED SERIES
When sexy detective—and *definitely* single man!—Nick Reed
returned home, he never guessed he'd be using his sleuthing skills to
clear Tabitha Harvey's name.

#716 MARRIED TO THE ENEMY—Ann Major
Embittered rancher Jonathan McBride never wanted to marry
again—and certainly not to Stormy Jones, the boss's daughter. So
why was he now tied to the one woman he'd vowed to avoid?

#717 ALMOST A BRIDE—Raye Morgan
Rafe Tennyson had convinced his brother to leave Kendall McCormick
waiting at the altar. But when he actually met the not-so-blushing
bride, he knew *his* bachelor days were numbered!

#718 NOT *HIS* WEDDING!—Suzanne Simms
Ross St. Clair had no time for any woman, but especially spoiled
heiresses like Diana Winsted. *Then* they were forced together and
their very lives depended on a dangerous charade....

#719 McCONNELL'S BRIDE—Naomi Horton
When Chase McConnell's wife died, he swore he'd never love again.
Yet when he needed an arranged marriage to keep his daughter, he
found himself falling for Prairie Skye, his "temporary" bride.

#720 BEST MAN FOR THE JOB—Dixie Browning
June's *Man of the Month* Rex Ryder and Carrie Lanier hunted
through the Carolinas to stop their runaway siblings from getting
married. But could the teenagers give *them* a lesson in love?

FREE GIFT OFFER

To receive your free gift, send us the specified number of proofs-of-purchase from any specially marked Free Gift Offer Harlequin or Silhouette book with the Free Gift Certificate properly completed, plus a check or money order (do not send cash) to cover postage and handling payable to Harlequin/Silhouette Free Gift Promotion Offer. We will send you the specified gift.

FREE GIFT CERTIFICATE

ITEM	A. GOLD TONE EARRINGS	B. GOLD TONE BRACELET	C. GOLD TONE NECKLACE
# of proofs-of-purchase required	3	6	9
Postage and Handling	$2.25	$2.75	$3.25
Check one	☐	☐	☐

Name: _____

Address: _____

City: _____ Province: _____ Postal Code: _____

Mail this certificate, specified number of proofs-of-purchase and a check or money order for postage and handling to: HARLEQUIN/SILHOUETTE FREE GIFT OFFER 1992, P.O. Box 622, Fort Erie, Ontario L2A 5X3. Requests must be received by July 31, 1992.

PLUS—Every time you submit a completed certificate with the correct number of proofs-of-purchase, you are automatically entered in our MILLION DOLLAR SWEEPSTAKES! No purchase or obligation necessary to enter. See below for alternate means of entry and how to obtain complete sweepstakes rules.

MILLION DOLLAR SWEEPSTAKES
NO PURCHASE OR OBLIGATION NECESSARY TO ENTER

To enter, hand-print (mechanical reproductions are not acceptable) your name and address on a 3"×5" card and mail to Million Dollar Sweepstakes 6097, c/o either P.O. Box 9056, Buffalo, NY 14269-9056 or P.O. Box 621, Fort Erie, Ontario L2A 5X3. Limit: one entry per envelope. Entries must be sent via 1st-class mail. For eligibility, entries must be received no later than March 31, 1994. No liability is assumed for printing errors, lost, late or misdirected entries.

Sweepstakes is open to persons 18 years of age or older. All applicable laws and regulations apply. Sweepstakes offer void wherever prohibited by law. Prizewinners will be determined no later than May 1994. Chances of winning are determined by the number of entries distributed and received. For a copy of the Official Rules governing this sweepstakes offer, send a self-addressed, stamped envelope (WA residents need not affix return postage) to: Million Dollar Sweepstakes Rules, P.O. Box 4733, Blair, NE 68009.

✂ SD2C

ONE PROOF-OF-PURCHASE

To collect your fabulous FREE GIFT you must include the necessary FREE GIFT proofs-of-purchase with a properly completed offer certificate.

(See inside back cover for offer details)